Sawyer leaned in. "I'll finish up here and maybe we can get out to the safe house before nightfall."

Even though he probably hadn't meant that to sound intimate, it did. This heat between them wasn't cooling down much.

He tore his gaze from Cassidy's and looked down at the baby. "You won't have to tend to her—"

"I want to," Cassidy interrupted.

"Just don't get too attached," he added. "If she's not mine, we'll need to find her parents."

"Too late. I'm already attached."

He mumbled, "Yeah," and brushed a kiss on the baby's cheek.

Then Cassidy's.

He leaned in and this time brushed a kiss on her mouth. There it was again. The trickle of heat that went from her lips to her toes.

SAWYER

USA TODAY Bestselling Author

DELORES FOSSEN

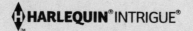

Recycling programs
for this product may
not exist in your area.

ISBN-13: 978-0-373-69758-8

SAWYER

Copyright © 2014 by Delores Fossen

Printed in U.S.A.

www.Harlequin.com

ABOUT THE AUTHOR

Imagine a family tree that includes Texas cowboys, Choctaw and Cherokee Indians, a Louisiana pirate and a Scottish rebel who battled side by side with William Wallace. With ancestors like that, it's easy to understand why *USA TODAY* bestselling author and former air force captain Delores Fossen feels as if she were genetically predisposed to writing romances. Along the way to fulfilling her DNA destiny, Delores married an air force top gun who just happens to be of Viking descent. With all those romantic bases covered, she doesn't have to look too far for inspiration.

Books by Delores Fossen

HARLEQUIN INTRIGUE

CAST OF CHARACTERS

Sawyer Ryland—A cowboy-lawman who's thrown into the middle of a dangerous kidnapping with an heiress and a newborn baby that might be his own.

Cassidy O'Neal—To free her brother from kidnappers, she must not only put herself in harm's way, but also she must join forces with Sawyer despite the bad blood between them.

Baby Emma—The newborn girl at the center of the kidnapping. But who are Emma's parents?

Bennie O'Neal—Cassidy's trouble-magnet brother who's keeping secrets from his sister.

April Warrick—A woman with a checkered past who might have orchestrated Bennie's kidnapping.

Willy Malloy—April's hotheaded ex-boyfriend. Did he help her with the kidnappings, or is he trying to make April look guilty?

Dr. Diane Blackwell—April's court-appointed therapist, but she might have a strong motive for the kidnapping.

Monica Barnes—A mystery woman from Sawyer's past who could reveal the truth about baby Emma.

Chapter One

Agent Sawyer Ryland caught the movement from the corner of his eye, turned and saw the blonde pushing her way through the other guests who'd gathered for the wedding reception.

She wasn't hard to spot.

She was practically running, and she had a bundle gripped in front of her like a shield.

Oh, mercy.

Sawyer's pulse kicked up a notch, and he automatically slid his hand inside his jacket and over his Glock. It was sad that his first response was to pull his firearm even at his own brother's wedding reception. Still, he'd been an FBI agent long enough—and had been shot too many times—that he lived by the code of better safe than sorry.

Or better safe than dead.

The woman didn't draw only Sawyer's attention. Nope. His brother, Josh, and their six Ryland cousins were all Silver Creek lawmen, and while Sawyer had his attention pinned on the woman, he was well aware that some of his cousins were reaching for their guns, too.

She stopped in the center of the barn, which had been decorated with hundreds of clear twinkling lights and flowers, and even though she was wearing dark sunglasses, Sawyer was pretty sure that her gaze rifled around. Obviously looking for someone. However, the looking around skidded to a halt when her attention landed on him.

"Sawyer," she said.

Because of the chattering guests and the fiddler sawing out some bluegrass, Sawyer didn't actually hear her speak his name. Instead, he saw it shape her trembling mouth. She yanked off the sunglasses, her gaze connecting with his.

And he cursed. Some really bad words.

For Pete's sake. He didn't need this today. Nor any other day for that matter.

"Cassidy O'Neal," he mumbled, and he made it sound like the profanity that he'd just spouted.

Yeah, it was her, all right. Except she didn't much look like a pampered princess doll today in her jeans and body-swallowing gray T-shirt. No makeup, either. Maybe he'd missed the memo about Hades freezing over, because Cassidy was not the sort to go without makeup, fine clothes or anything else *fine,* for that matter.

Despite the fact that he wasn't giving off any welcoming vibes whatsoever, Cassidy hurried to him. Her mouth was still trembling. Her dark green eyes rapidly blinking. There were beads of sweat on her forehead and upper lip despite the half dozen or so massive fans circulating air into the barn.

"I'm sorry," she said, and she thrust whatever she was carrying at him.

Sawyer didn't take it and backed up, but not before he caught a glimpse of the tiny hand gripping the white blanket.

A baby.

That put his heart right in his suddenly dry throat.

He'd always been darn good at math. Not now though.

Not with the air just sucked right out of his lungs. But he didn't need to do the math to know that while there was no love lost between Cassidy and him, there had been love.

Or rather, sex.

It wasn't love by any stretch of the imagination.

Using just his index finger, Sawyer eased back the blanket and saw the curly mop of brown hair on the sleeping baby's head. A lighter color than his own hair but maybe a mix of Cassidy's and his. A cherub face that resembled every baby he'd ever seen.

Including his own cousins' babies.

And there were plenty of them around for him to do a split-second comparison.

"No." Cassidy shook her head so hard that her ponytail came unhooked and her hair dropped against her shoulders. "The baby's not mine."

Not mine.

Which meant it wasn't his, either.

That gave him a much-needed jolt of breath to stop his head from going light. A light head was hardly the right bargaining tool for a lawman, and even though Sawyer had no idea if what was going on would require any of his lawman skills, he figured he'd at least need to be able to think straight for this.

Sawyer wasn't the only one with breathing issues. Cassidy's was gusting now, and she pushed the bundled baby toward him again. "You have to take her."

Again, Sawyer backed up.

"Is there a problem?" someone growled.

It was his cousin Mason, a deputy sheriff of Silver Creek and possibly the most unfriendly looking person on earth.

And he walked up right behind Sawyer.

When Mason and he were kids, people used to say

they looked like twins, and their combined badass presence, glares and scowls should have been enough to deter a wedding-crashing heiress from staying put.

It didn't.

"I don't have much time," Cassidy insisted. "You have to take her, and I have to get a picture of you holding her."

Mason and Sawyer exchanged a glance. They were on the same page in thinking their visitor was a couple of cans short of a six-pack.

"We have to talk," Cassidy continued, and she freed her other hand from the baby bundle so she could catch onto Sawyer's arm. "Please," she added.

Sawyer had known Cassidy on and off for over a year now. Mostly off. But he'd never heard her say please. And he'd never seen that look of pure fear in her eyes. He pushed her hand off his arm and instead caught onto her wrist.

"I'll be right back," he told Mason. "Obviously our visitor and I need to have a word."

"You know what you're doing?" Mason asked.

Nope. But Sawyer figured he was about to find out something he didn't want to know. Actually, anything that Cassidy had to say to him would fall into that *didn't want to know* category even if she hadn't been carrying a baby in her arms.

Sawyer led her back through the crowd, weaving in and out of the kids running around and the couples dancing. Nearly every one of his cousins shot him a glance to make sure he was okay, and Sawyer tried not to respond with anything that would cause the party to end. His brother Josh, and his bride, Jaycee, didn't deserve to have their happy day spoiled.

There was a storm brewing, and it was just starting to drizzle, so Sawyer didn't pull Cassidy out into the open.

Instead, he took her to a long watering trough that had a tin awning overhead.

"Let's start with some questions," he told Cassidy. "I ask them and you answer them," he snapped when she opened her mouth to interrupt him.

Of course she just continued with that interruption. "We don't have time for a Q and A."

"Obviously, you missed the part about me asking the questions. Make time."

It hit Sawyer then. Even though Cassidy had said the baby wasn't hers, that didn't mean he'd leaped to the right conclusion about the little one not being *his*. He hadn't been seriously involved with anyone in several years, but there had been some short hookups. Like the attorney in San Antonio and the woman he'd met at a party.

Was the timing right for either of them?

He just didn't know.

He looked in the blanket again. At that little cherub face. At the hair. "Is she mine?"

No more gusting breath for Cassidy. It just streamed from her mouth, and she shook her head again. "I have no idea."

Well, that didn't help.

Sawyer wasn't exactly proud of the fact that he didn't know if he'd fathered a child.

Time for some direct questions. "Who is she, and where'd you get her?" Sawyer demanded.

"I honestly don't have time for this." She looked over her shoulder at the beat-up blue truck just a few yards away. There were more dents and dings on it than smooth surface, and the roof was blistered with rust. The engine was running. The wipers, still going. It was hardly her usual ride, but then nothing about this little visit could be labeled as *usual* for Cassidy.

Sawyer cupped her chin, lifted it, forcing eye contact. "Where. Did. You. Get. The. Baby?" Best to slow down his words and see if that helped.

"From two men. They were both wearing cartoon masks and they were armed."

Now, that was an answer he sure as heck hadn't expected. He drew his gun and positioned himself in front of Cassidy. Even if she was lying—and he couldn't figure out why she'd do that—he had to treat this like a crime in progress.

"Did the men bring you here to the ranch?" he asked.

"No. I drove in the truck they told me to use." She huffed, glanced at the phone she had clutched in her left hand. "They gave me the baby, said to bring her to you and take a picture of you holding her. I'm supposed to leave the baby with you and then get back so I can give them the picture."

Say what? That still didn't make a lick of sense.

"Where are these men?" Sawyer went on full alert, his gaze firing all around the grounds. And it was a lot of ground to cover. What didn't help was there were guests coming and going, and there were vehicles parked everywhere.

"I don't know." Cassidy's eyes were wild, a different kind of storm brewing there, and every muscle in her body was rock hard.

Sawyer got right in her face. "The sooner you answer me, the sooner I can help. Where are these men, and where are you supposed to meet them?"

"I don't know," she repeated. "They said they'd call me in thirty minutes and tell me where to drop off the photo. It's already past the time." Her voice broke, and a hoarse sob tore from her throat.

Okay. He could add sheer terror to her panic. That

wasn't helping his own reactions, and while Sawyer wanted to know if this child was his, he needed to figure out if any danger was imminent.

"So, you don't know who the men are?" Not sure he believed that, but he pressed for details. He figured the devil was in those. "How'd you meet them?"

"I didn't *meet* them. They kidnapped me two days ago and have been holding me blindfolded."

All right. So, there had been a crime, and he believed her—about that anyway. It was hard to fake that kind of body language, the broken breath and the sob.

But he immediately rethought that.

This was Cassidy, and she'd lied to him before. In fact, it was the reason their very brief affair had ended. And it was that reminder that caused his stomach to start churning.

"Does this have anything to do with your brother?" he asked. Except Sawyer didn't just ask. He demanded it.

She swallowed hard. Nodded. "Yes." It was one of the first direct answers she'd given him since her arrival, and it wasn't a good time for it.

"Bennie's behind this," Sawyer grumbled, and he would have cursed some more, but he didn't want to do that in front of the baby.

Bennie, her low-life, scheming younger brother. There were about a hundred more labels he could have slapped on the idiot, but the bottom line was that Bennie was really bad news. Always one step ahead of the law and the crooks that he dealt with. And big sis, Cassidy, was always there to bail him out.

But if the baby was Sawyer's, then why the heck was Bennie involved?

He didn't have an answer to that, either. Yet.

Cassidy's phone rang, the sound shooting through his

thoughts. He didn't have to tell her to answer it. Bobbling the baby in her arms, Cassidy fumbled to press the answer button. Sawyer hadn't really planned on it, but he took the child so Cassidy wouldn't drop her, and he waited. The first thing he saw was the blocked caller ID on the screen.

Not a good sign.

Even though his entire focus should have been on the call, he glanced down at the baby again. Soon, very soon, he'd have to know the truth about her paternity. For now, he pressed the speaker button on Cassidy's phone so he could hear what the caller was saying.

"You got the picture?" the man on the phone growled.

"I'm getting it," Cassidy assured him. "What about my brother? Where is he? *How* is he?"

"You'll get to see him as soon as you bring us back that picture."

Sawyer huffed. "Genius, she wants proof that her brother's still alive," he spelled out to the person on the other end of the line. He didn't bother to take the sarcasm out of his voice, either. "Now, here's the part where you provide that proof, or this conversation ends."

Silence. For a long time.

Grabbing on to his jacket sleeve, Cassidy frantically shook her head. Probably because she wanted him to stay quiet.

Sawyer ignored that.

In the next couple of minutes, he was going to have to ignore a lot of head-shaking and just about anything that she was saying. Because there was no way he was going to let her leave to face these kidnappers alone—no matter how much proof of life they provided.

There was some mumbling and cussing on the other

end of the line. "Here he is," the man snapped, and the phone dinged, indicating there was a message.

Cassidy hit the button, and a moment later the video loaded. There was Bennie, all right. His hands were tied with a rope to what appeared to be wooden beams on a ceiling. He was stretched out like a moth in a science experiment.

"Oh, God." Cassidy pressed her fingers to her mouth, but she didn't manage to silence the gasp. "You've hurt him."

Sawyer had to agree with her on that point. His face was bloody and bruised, as if he'd taken a good beating. His hair was matted, maybe with more blood, and even though he was moving and mumbling, he looked like a man on the verge of losing consciousness.

Or dying.

"Why are they doing this to you?" Sawyer asked Bennie.

But just like that, the video ended. "That's all the proof you'll get. Now, it's your turn. Get that photo here," the caller demanded. "You got thirty minutes, or we finish him off."

"Why?" Sawyer repeated. He needed to keep them talking. Needed to find out their location and anything else he could learn about them. He spotted his cousin, Sheriff Grayson Ryland, in the doorway of the barn, and Sawyer motioned for him to come over.

But Grayson had barely made it a step when there was a flash of light. Since his body was on full alert, it took Sawyer a second to realize that it had come from the camera.

Cassidy had snapped his picture.

With the baby.

"I'm so sorry," she said, and Cassidy took off running.

Chapter Two

Cassidy didn't look back, but she could hear Sawyer cursing at her and shouting for her to stop. A moment later, she heard more than just his voice.

She heard footsteps. Someone running. And she had no doubt that it was Sawyer coming after her.

Her heart was past the racing stage now. Breath, too. And her hands were shaking so hard that she was surprised and relieved when she managed to open the truck door. She jumped in and immediately threw the gear into Reverse. She had to get out of there now and get the photo back to those men.

The images of her brother's battered face flew through her head. Images of the shock on Sawyer's face, too, when she'd handed him the baby. Later, if there was a later, she'd need to deal with him.

Except *later* came a lot sooner than she'd planned.

She felt the thud and looked into the rearview mirror to see that Sawyer had jumped into the truck bed.

Mercy.

She didn't need this.

He no longer had the baby. He'd obviously handed the newborn off to the other man who'd been approaching them when Cassidy had snapped the picture. And now that Sawyer's hands were free, he was making his way from the back of the truck bed and toward her. If looks could kill, that glare he shot her would have hurtled her to the hereafter.

Still, Cassidy didn't stop. In fact, she slammed her foot on the accelerator and threaded the truck through the sea of other vehicles. Not the best time to attempt something like this with all the partygoers around, but she hadn't exactly had a choice.

She didn't want to hurt Sawyer, but she couldn't have him go to the kidnappers with her, either. Earlier, they'd warned her if she didn't return alone, her brother would die. That couldn't happen. She couldn't lose Bennie.

The moment that she was in a small clearing, Cassidy jerked the steering wheel to the right to try to toss Sawyer off the back. It didn't work. He held on, and it only made his glare a whole lot worse. Still, she tried again.

Again, no luck.

Sawyer held on, bouncing around on the metal surface of the truck bed. He managed to hang on to his gun, and she was afraid he might use it on her if he got the chance. He already hated her, and this certainly wasn't going to make things better between them.

Cassidy sped across the driveway that coiled around the sprawling main house and the barns, and she finally reached the ranch road that would take her to the highway. She'd lied when she told Sawyer she didn't know where the kidnappers were.

A necessary lie.

If he had learned their location, he'd just go in there with guns blazing, and Bennie would be caught in the middle of a firefight. Of course, that might still happen if she couldn't ditch Sawyer before she made it to the abandoned building where they were holding her brother.

Cassidy tried again to toss him from the truck, but she

failed that time, too. Sawyer not only held on, he made his way toward her. Inch by inch.

There was a small slider window that separated them. Not nearly big enough for him to crawl through, and it had a lock that would prevent anyone on the outside from opening it. Thank goodness. Still, that didn't solve her problem of getting rid of him.

She was already going too fast, and as if fate and Mother Nature were working against her, the drizzle turned to a hard rain, making the road even more slick than it already was. Cassidy tried to focus on her driving. On ditching Sawyer. And getting this photo to the kidnappers.

But Sawyer obviously had other ideas about the ditching part.

He lifted his gun, took aim. Not at her. He aimed the barrel of his gun at the passenger's window.

"No!" Cassidy shouted.

Too late.

He turned his head and fired, the shot blasting through not just both windows—the side and back—but the sound seemed to rip through her, too. Her heart slammed against her ribs, and she hit the brakes. Not the best idea she'd ever had, but it was hard to make a good decision with the pain from the noise crashing through her ears and head.

The truck tires fishtailed on the wet asphalt, slinging Sawyer and her around. Even though she was wearing her seat belt, her shoulder slammed so hard into her door that she swore she saw stars. She certainly lost her breath.

Unlike Sawyer.

The truck hadn't even come to a full stop yet when he reached through the gaping hole in the safety glass on the passenger's side and unlocked the door. Opened it. As if it were a routine maneuver for him, he slid from the truck bed and into the cab.

He put his gun to her head.

"You will tell me what's going on *now*," he growled. His glare was even worse, and the tendons in his neck corded.

"I've already told you all I know." She tried to sound tough as nails, like him. And she failed miserably. She wasn't tough. She was terrified, exhausted and just wanted this ordeal to end. "Now, get out."

"Not gonna happen."

There it was. That smart mouth that she used to think was funny and a complement to his bad-boy persona. It had been the very thing that had lured her to him. But his mouth and his tenacity weren't much of a lure now. Nothing was.

Well, except for that brief slap of attraction she'd felt when she first saw him in the barn.

That slap might have to be a real one that she delivered to herself, because an attraction to Sawyer should be the last thing on her mind.

"They'll kill Bennie if you're with me," she reminded him. Somehow, she got the truck moving again because like everything else, time wasn't working in her favor.

He shook his head, cursed her again and slung the water off his face. It didn't help. The rain coming in from the window just walloped him once more, soaking his jacket, white shirt and jeans. His hair, too. The drops of water slid off those dark brown strands and dripped onto his face.

"Who says they won't just kill you when you give them the photo?" he asked. "You should have taken this to the cops and not tried to handle it yourself."

"I didn't go to the cops because they said they'd kill Bennie."

"Kidnappers always say that," he snapped. "And they always tell the mark to cooperate and that you'll get your loved one back in one piece. Maybe you will, maybe you won't. But they could just as easily put a bullet in you as Bennie."

Obviously, he thought she was stupid.

"They won't do that because I haven't given them all the ransom money yet, that's why. The other half won't be transferred to their account until Bennie and I are away from the pick-up site. And I'm the only one with the bank account information. If they kill me, they don't get the other half million."

He mumbled something she didn't catch. "You're paying a million dollars' ransom for your brother?"

"You'd do the same for your brother."

"Yeah. Because he's a good guy and not some low-life weasel. What'd Bennie do this time to get himself in this mess?"

"I don't know." Her voice cracked, and she could feel what little composure she had cracking, too. "At this point, it doesn't matter. Bennie's the only family I have, and I'll give them every penny I own to get him back."

And while a million wasn't every penny she owned, it was close. It would wipe her out financially, but there was no way she could live with herself if she hadn't agreed to the kidnappers' every demand.

Including that photo.

"Is the baby yours?" she asked. Cassidy took the turn too fast toward the town of Silver Creek, and the tires squealed on the road.

"I don't know," Sawyer said after several long moments. He slung off more water, swiveled in the seat and looked around.

"You don't know if you had sex with a woman about ten months ago?" Cassidy pressed.

Yes, she sounded irked about that. And was. She'd always been attracted to the bad-boy types, but it never felt good to know that she was in a mountain-high pile of women that Sawyer had discarded.

Even if she'd contributed a lot to the reason he'd discarded her.

"There's someone," he admitted. "I'll call her as soon as I'm finished with this. But I'm pretty sure if she'd gotten pregnant, she would have told me." And he took out his phone. "I'm calling my cousin, the sheriff."

"No!" Even though she had to take one of her hands off the steering wheel, Cassidy did it so she could grab his phone. "No cops. No anyone but me."

He leaned in, a major violation of her personal space. So close she could smell wedding cake on his breath. "I'm going to the drop site with you. Close your mouth," he added when she opened it. "Because arguing won't help. You're taking me to those kidnappers so I can find out why they want the photo. And why they took Bennie."

Sawyer fired off a text message. Probably requesting backup that could make this mess a thousand times worse.

"I could stop the truck and refuse to go there," she lied.

And the flat look Sawyer gave her with those blistering blue eyes let her know that he, too, knew she was lying.

"Where's this place?" He sounded like the tough FBI agent that he was.

"Just off Miller's Road." She checked the time on

the dash clock. "And I have less than ten minutes to get there."

"Where on Miller's Road?" Sawyer didn't address that time was ticking away, either.

"It's an abandoned building." Now she was the one to get in his face. For a brief glare, anyway. "Don't you dare make me regret telling you."

"Abandoned," he repeated. "The Tumbleweed? It used to be a bar."

She nodded. The sign had been rusted and battered, but the name was still partially visible. "You know the place?"

"Yeah." And that one word held a lot of emotion. Or something. "I was raised in Silver Creek. The Tumbleweed used to belong to my grandfather."

Oh, mercy. Cassidy doubted that was a coincidence. "So, what does Bennie's kidnapping have to do with you?"

Sawyer lifted his shoulder. "Like I said, that's what I intend to find out. Take that next left."

"That's not Miller's Road."

"I know. And that's why we're taking it. Turn!" he growled.

It was the second time in the past few moments that she'd hoped she didn't regret this, but Cassidy took the turn. It wasn't a road but an old ranch trail with thick underbrush on both sides. Not exactly a good driving surface with the rain, and the first pothole she hit made the truck bounce, and their heads struck the ceiling.

"Slow down and stop up there," Sawyer instructed, and he pointed to a pile of limestone boulders.

Again, she did as he said, but the moment she stopped, Cassidy took hold of his jacket and forced eye contact. "I know you think Bennie doesn't deserve to live, but swear to me that you won't do anything to make this worse."

His eyes narrowed. "I'm an FBI agent, sworn to uphold the law. That includes upholding it for people who don't deserve it. Like your brother. Now, kill the engine and wait here."

As if she would take that order as gospel, which she did, Sawyer stepped from the truck, his gun ready, and he climbed to the top of the boulders.

Cassidy couldn't be sure, but she thought that Miller's Road might be just on the other side. She'd been so frantic when she'd driven out of there earlier with the baby, that the only thing she had paid attention to was the GPS that the kidnappers had programmed with the directions to the Ryland family's Silver Creek ranch.

What the two men hadn't told her was there would be a wedding reception going on and that she'd have to get that photo with dozens of witnesses milling around. But certainly the kidnappers must have known because they'd told her that's where she would find Sawyer.

So, why take the photo there?

Too many things about this didn't make sense, and that was yet more reason to get Bennie away from these men.

"I have less than five minutes now," she reminded him in a whisper.

Sawyer didn't respond to that, fired off another text, and then without warning, he scrambled over the rocks, out of sight. That got Cassidy moving from the truck, and she hurried to the boulders to see where he'd gone.

She didn't have to look far.

He was there, just on the other side, crouched down by yet another heap of boulders. Beyond that was the road.

Then, the Tumbleweed bar about fifty yards away.

It wasn't much of a place. Rust-streaked tin roof.

Weathered clapboards. Eye-socket windows with vines coiling in and out of them. What was left of the neon sign was connected by a single electrical wire, and it creaked back and forth with each gust of wind.

Sawyer gave her a stare down even though he was looking up at her. "Think hard. Do you remember me telling you to wait in the truck?" He didn't give her a chance to respond. "Because that's exactly what you're going to do. My cousin Grayson will be here soon to watch you."

She huffed. "I don't want a babysitter. I want to help."

"And you'll do that by waiting here." He tipped his head to the building. "No vehicles. Were there any when you left?"

"No. They brought me here in the truck. They already had Bennie tied up inside."

It hurt just to think of seeing him that way. To see the terror on his face. To know that he'd seen the same on hers. She was the big sister. Had always taken care of him just as she'd promised.

This time, she'd failed.

Sawyer started to move but then stopped and caught her gaze. "If you follow me, it could get all of us killed. Nod so I know you understand."

Her stomach twisted, the acid rising to her throat. But she nodded. "Please, hurry," she begged. "Save him."

Sawyer scowled as if insulted that she had to ask, and he put his hand on the top of the boulders to lever himself up. However, he didn't make it an inch before they heard the sound. A sound that Cassidy definitely didn't want to hear.

A bloodcurdling scream.

Chapter Three

Sawyer had to take hold of Cassidy to keep her from bolting toward the building. He had to fight his own instincts, too, because that scream was the sound of someone terrified.

Maybe even dying.

"We have to help him," Cassidy insisted.

And there was another scream. Like the first one, it didn't sound like a man's, either.

"Who else was in that building?" Sawyer demanded, and because she was still in fight mode, he had to snap her to him so that her face was just a few inches from his.

Cassidy was breathing through her mouth now, her chest pumping, and she shook her head. "No one that I saw."

The third scream got to him. Since Grayson wasn't there yet and because he knew for a fact that Cassidy wouldn't stay put, Sawyer shoved her behind him. "If I tell you to get down, you'll do it," he barked.

Whether she would was anyone's guess, but he couldn't wait while a woman was murdered. Heck, it could be the baby's mother.

Sawyer didn't waste any time getting Cassidy across the narrow dirt road. The mud caked on the soles of his boots, but he forced himself to run. Cassidy ran, too, despite the flimsy flip-flops she was wearing. They darted behind some trees, using them for cover so he could make his way to the Tumbleweed.

He knew every inch of the place and thought back to the video he'd seen of Bennie. It had been dark, but the only part of the building with beams like the ones he'd seen were in the main bar. Or rather what was left of it. Time and vandals had taken their toll.

Cassidy tapped her phone screen where the time was displayed. Yeah, he knew they were down to seconds now, but they couldn't just go charging in there.

He led her to the side of the building and to what had once been the private entrance to his grandfather's office. There was no door now, just a dark hole of a room. Sawyer stepped inside, pulled Cassidy in behind him and listened.

No more screams.

Just the creepy sounds of the wind and the rain pushing and squealing through the sliver-thin gaps in the wood.

Cassidy tapped the time again and put her hand on his back to push him forward. He went, but clearly not at the breakneck, run-into-a-trap pace that she wanted. Sawyer paused again in the doorway that led into the bar itself and peered inside.

"No," he warned her. Cassidy would have rushed straight into the room if Sawyer hadn't stopped her.

There was enough light spearing through the holes in the roof and windows that Sawyer could see the room was empty. So were the ropes that dangled from the exposed ceiling beams.

"Bennie was right here when I left," she said, the words gusting out with her breath. "We're too late."

Maybe. But Sawyer doubted the kidnappers would

just walk away from half a million dollars. Keeping his gun ready, he started to the center of the room. Toward those ropes.

With each step, the debris, dead insects and God knows what else crunched beneath his boots. Along with the rain bulleting on the tin roof and the other sounds from the storm, it made it hard to hear footsteps or anything else to indicate the kidnappers' location.

Cassidy stayed plastered against his back, literally breathing down his neck, and they approached the ropes together.

Sawyer cursed.

First, when he spotted what was on the ropes. Then again, when he stepped in a puddle of dark liquid. With his luck, he figured that wasn't rainwater from the leaky roof.

Nope.

It was blood.

"They hurt him," Cassidy mumbled, and she pressed her fingers to her mouth. No doubt to suppress the sob.

Sawyer felt for her. If that were his brother's blood, he'd be ready to panic, too, but panicking wasn't going to help Bennie.

He passed her his phone. "Text Grayson and tell him we're inside the Tumbleweed and that your brother's missing."

Her hands were shaking, so it wasn't a speedy process for her to type the message, but she finally did it, and he heard the little dinging sound to indicate it had been sent.

"We have to find him," Cassidy insisted. "He probably needs a doctor."

Yeah. If he was still alive. But Sawyer kept that possibility to himself and double-checked the room. It was one big open space, the tables and chair long since removed so there weren't many places for two kidnappers and their hostage to hide.

That meant they'd likely gone outside.

Of course they had.

Over the years, the woods had closed in on the place so it was hard to even tell that there had once been a parking lot back there. Since he hadn't seen anyone on the road itself and no one was here, it was likely the kidnappers' escape route.

Cassidy must have figured that out, too, because she bolted around him, heading straight for the rickety-looking double doors that led out back. One of them was completely off its hinges and propped against the jamb. The other, however, was closed just enough to conceal someone who might be lurking around.

Sawyer snagged her by the shoulder and put her behind him again. He also tossed her a glare, hopefully a reminder that she was playing by his rules. And his rules didn't involve her running out there until he was sure they weren't about to be gunned down. He'd heard no shot to go along with those screams, but that didn't mean the kidnappers wouldn't pull their triggers.

Taking slow, cautious steps, Sawyer went to the remaining door. Took aim and made a quick check.

No one was there.

He glanced around, looking for any sign of the men, and he soon found it. Even though the rain was quickly washing it away, there was blood on the ground, and the underbrush had been stomped down in spots. It left a visible trail that led deeper into the woods.

His phone dinged, and since Cassidy was still holding it, she looked at the screen. "Grayson will be here in five minutes," she relayed. "That's too long. I want to find my brother now."

Five minutes was indeed a long time for someone who might be bleeding out. "Text Grayson to get an ambulance out here."

That sent her breath gusting again, but she did as he said. Sawyer did something, too. He ignored that warning knot in his gut. The one that told him it wasn't a bright idea to go in the woods with Cassidy in tow, but it was too dangerous to leave her behind.

Too risky for Bennie not to be rescued.

So, the warning knot lost out, and Sawyer moved forward. Listening and praying this wasn't a decision that would get them killed.

Cassidy put her forearms against his back, pushing him. Or rather she was trying to do that. But Sawyer held his pace steady, looking for any evidence that the rain would soon destroy. If they didn't find Bennie soon, they'd need any and all clues to figure out where the kidnappers had taken him.

But why had they moved him?

Had they spotted Sawyer and decided to run? Or maybe Bennie had tried to escape. If he'd managed to get loose from those ropes, he could have run. And maybe he'd been hurt in the process.

Sawyer maneuvered them several yards deeper. Stopped and listened. This time, he heard something other than Cassidy's breathing and the rain slapping at them.

It was just a swish of a sound. But not like anything else that he'd heard since this little trek had begun. Sawyer pulled Cassidy beneath the sagging branches of a mesquite and waited.

He didn't have to wait long.

There was another of those swishing sounds, but this time he heard it a whole lot clearer. Oh, man. Someone had fired a gun rigged with a silencer. It was hard to tell the exact origin of the shots, but they hadn't come from behind them.

Definitely ahead.

"Gunshots," Sawyer whispered to Cassidy when she kept pushing him to get moving.

That stopped her. But it didn't stop the fear from rising inside her. Sawyer could feel that in her tightened muscles and trembling hands.

"Send Grayson another text to give him our location," he told her.

That would get her mind on something other than the panic that was no doubt about to eat her alive. Still, the texting served a necessary purpose, too. He didn't want his cousin walking into gunfire.

There were no more swishing sounds, but Sawyer heard something else that grabbed his attention.

A moan.

Definitely human, and with the blood they'd found, it had likely come from someone injured. Bennie, maybe. At least that meant he was alive.

For now anyway.

Cassidy must have heard the sound, too, because she nudged him to get moving again. Sawyer did, maneuvering from beneath the mesquite and to some thick underbrush that would hopefully give them enough cover if those kidnappers started shooting at them.

There was a small clearing ahead, and because there were no trees, the rain was soaking the ground, making it hard to tell if anyone had gone that way. If the kidnappers had learned their way around these woods, and Sawyer had to assume that they had, they would know there were two ways out.

Doubling back to Miller's Road.

Or continuing through the woods about a mile until they reached an old farm road.

Since he hadn't seen another vehicle, it was possible the kidnappers had parked on that farm road. Of course, it was risky to be so far away from transportation in case something went wrong.

And something obviously had.

They likely hadn't wanted to shoot at a hostage when they were so close to getting their hands on the entire chunk of ransom money.

"Bennie and the woman have to be alive," Cassidy mumbled, and her breathing got even faster.

Mercy. She was on the verge of hyperventilating now, and Sawyer reached behind him and touched his fingers to her lips. Cassidy jerked back as if he'd burnt her. Their gazes met. Not one of those ordinary meets, either. This was one of blasted nonverbal connections between a man and a woman.

Who'd once been lovers.

Not a good time to remember that. Never a good time, actually. And he scowled to let her know that.

She scowled, too, her eyes narrowing a bit, and just like that, he'd cured her panic attack and hyperventilating.

"Let's find him," Cassidy snarled, and considering she'd just whispered it, she'd done a thorough job in conveying that snarl.

Her gaze fired around. "I have the picture," Cassidy shouted without warning.

Sawyer reeled to her so fast that his neck popped. "What the heck are you doing?" he mouthed.

"Giving them what they want," she mouthed back, her teeth clenched.

"If they'd wanted the photo bad enough, the kidnappers would have hung around." And maybe they had. If so, Cassidy had just given away their position.

So, Sawyer moved again, trying hard not to let his anger turn what should be quiet footsteps into stomps. They'd only made it a few feet when he heard another moan. It was weak, barely audible, but it had come from a clump of cedars about fifteen yards away.

But that wasn't the only sound.

There were footsteps that even the rain couldn't conceal. Sawyer froze, holding back Cassidy again, but he didn't have to hold her for long. There was a blur of motion, and Sawyer automatically took aim.

It was someone running.

Someone dressed all in dark clothes who quickly darted out of sight. In the video, Bennie had been wearing a light colored T-shirt similar to the one Cassidy had on.

The runner had to be one of the kidnappers.

There were more footsteps. Not from the same direction where the runner had disappeared to, but on the opposite side of the clearing. It wasn't the running pace of an injured man who was hurt enough to moan. This was another runner.

And likely the second kidnapper.

Sawyer cursed himself for bringing Cassidy into this. Of course, if he'd left her to wait for Grayson, she would have no doubt been another set of those fast-moving footsteps trudging around in the rainy woods.

The seconds crawled by while he waited and tried to figure out what the heck was going on. He certainly couldn't just start shooting with Bennie out there.

Behind him, he heard more footsteps. Not a runner this time, but the slow, cautious steps of a lawman. Sawyer glanced over his shoulder and spotted Grayson.

He motioned to the clearing so that Grayson would know what he was about to do.

"Stay here," he warned Cassidy, and Grayson moved closer to her.

Good. If bullets started flying, Grayson would be able to pull her to the ground.

Sawyer tightened his grip on his gun and stepped out, making a beeline toward the cedars where he'd heard the moaning. No moans now, which might mean the kidnappers had moved their injured hostage.

When he reached the cedars, Sawyer used his elbow to push aside some of the branches. The first thing he saw was more blood.

And lots of it.

It had mixed with rainwater, making it impossible to tell just how much, but the bleeder had left a trail for him to follow.

No more footsteps. Just the sound of his own heartbeat crashing in his ears.

Sawyer pushed back another cedar branch, and he cursed when he saw the lifeless body on the ground in front of him.

Chapter Four

"No!" Cassidy blurted out. Nothing could have stopped her from running to Sawyer.

And toward the person lying on the ground.

Sawyer stooped down, touched his fingers to the person's neck and shook his head. "Dead."

Her heart was practically beating out of her chest by the time she made it there, and she tried to brace herself for the worst. Unfortunately, she wasn't sure she could handle the worst.

Sawyer took hold of her to stop her from going closer, but she still got a good look at the person lying on the ground.

Not Bennie.

The victim was a woman with jaggedly chopped hair, black with streaks of blue. Cassidy had no idea who she was, but she had no trouble seeing the bullet wound on the side of her head.

Despite the gruesome scene, the relief was instant and overwhelming. It robbed her of what little breath she had left. But the relief was also short lived. It wasn't Bennie. But where was he?

"Bennie?" she yelled.

No answer. Nothing.

Cassidy would have bolted again to go look for him,

but Sawyer stopped her. "Who is she?" He tipped his head to the woman on the ground.

"I don't know." Again, she tried to leave, and Sawyer stopped her.

"You're not going anywhere," he insisted. "The kidnappers have already killed one woman. You want to make it two?"

"I want to find my brother," she insisted right back.

"We'll do that. Come on. This is a crime scene now, and it needs to be processed. That's our best bet at finding Bennie."

Maybe. But everything inside her was screaming for her to run and find her brother. Even if she knew it wasn't the logical thing to do.

"Something obviously went wrong here," Sawyer said as he led her away from the body. "But the kidnappers will contact you again. They'll keep Bennie alive because they want to get that ransom."

That made it through the panic and the haze in her head. Yes, the kidnappers wanted the money. She had to believe that, hold on to it. Because it was the only way to keep herself sane.

Sawyer and she approached Sheriff Grayson Ryland, and he handed Sawyer a set of keys. "Use my truck and get her to the hospital so she can be checked out. I already have an ambulance and CSI team on the way."

"The woman's dead," Sawyer told him.

The sheriff looked as if he wanted to curse, and he made another call. This time to the medical examiner.

"Please let me know if the men come back with Bennie," she said to the sheriff.

He nodded, continued his call, and Sawyer got her moving toward a silver pickup parked just up the road.

Not a slow pace, either. They were practically jogging, and he kept watch, his gaze firing all around.

Cassidy doubted the kidnappers would kill her. But she rethought that. She'd broken their rules by not returning with the photo in time.

Was that the reason they'd killed the woman?

The emotion was already high, boiling through her, and that caused her to gasp. "Did the kidnappers kill her to punish me?" she managed to ask.

Sawyer didn't answer because he obviously didn't know. He stuffed her into the truck, got behind the wheel and drove out of there fast.

"I don't need to go to the hospital," she told him. "I'm okay. Or at least I will be when we find Bennie."

"It's standard practice to be checked out. After all, you were kidnapped."

Yes, and she was rattled, but there wasn't a scratch on her. She knew after seeing that video that Bennie wouldn't be able to say the same thing. Those men had clearly hurt him.

"Don't try to make sense of this," Sawyer warned her after glancing at her face. "Let's just get an ID on the body and go from there."

It didn't seem nearly enough, not with Bennie's life at stake. Still, she knew Sawyer was right. They couldn't go blindly running in the woods looking for him.

"But what does that woman have to do with the kidnapping and my brother?" she asked.

"Maybe she was one of the kidnappers."

Cassidy was about to disagree, but the truth was, she had no idea if anyone else was involved. "I only saw the two men with cartoon masks."

He spared her another glance before his eyes went back to the road. "And you're sure they were both men?"

Was she? Well, she had been until Sawyer had asked that question. "Only one of them spoke, and it was definitely a man. But even if the other one was a woman, why would he have killed her?"

"Maybe because he didn't want to split the ransom money with her. It happens all the time. Despite the cliché, there's not much honor among thieves."

He was right, and the kidnapper could now be a killer. A killer who had her brother.

Even though it wasn't cold, she was soaking wet, and Cassidy began to shiver. Sawyer noticed, turned on the heat, and he sped up the wipers, too. It didn't help much. The rain was coming down even harder now, and the wipers couldn't keep up with the downpour.

"This is destroying the crime scene, isn't it?" Cassidy asked.

He lifted his shoulder, kept his gaze pinned to the road. "Grayson's a good sheriff. If there's anything to find, he'll find it."

She thought about that a moment, trying to piece together this puzzle. "They held Bennie and me in your grandfather's bar. Why? Why would they believe you and I have a connection?"

Another lift of his shoulder, but that wasn't a casual response she saw in his eyes. No way. He was troubled by all of this—especially about the baby that she'd photographed in his arms.

Why would the kidnappers have wanted that?

She was about to ask him, but his phone buzzed, and she saw Grayson's name on the screen. Cassidy held her breath, waiting and praying again that this wasn't bad news about her brother.

"The dead woman had a wallet in her pants pocket," she heard Grayson say. Since the call wasn't on speaker, she scooted closer to Sawyer so she could listen to every word. "According to her driver's license, her name is April Warrick."

Cassidy repeated it, hoping it would spark some kind of recognition. It didn't.

"I'm having someone run a background on her now," the sheriff added.

"Good, we're almost at the hospital. After Cassidy sees the doctor, I can help get all of this sorted out. What about the baby?" Sawyer asked. "Any calls about her? Is she okay?"

"She's still with Mason at the E.R.—where you told him to take her. He says the baby's fine, that he's just waiting on the paperwork."

That was something at least. Cassidy hated the thought of an innocent baby being put in the middle of this mess.

"I told Mason to have the doctors do blood and DNA tests on the baby," Sawyer added.

Grayson stayed quiet a moment. "You want the DNA compared to yours?"

"Yeah." Sawyer paused, too. "And if I'm not a match, then I'll run it through the system to see if we can find out who is."

She wasn't sure what to hope for. At least if the child were Sawyer's, then she would have him to protect her.

"Any sign of Bennie?" Cassidy asked. She moved even closer to Sawyer, until they were shoulder to shoulder. He noticed, glanced down at the contact between them and scowled. But Cassidy stayed put.

"Nothing yet," Grayson answered, and with that, Sawyer did hang up. Another glance at her had Cassidy moving back to her side of the seat.

"You still haven't forgiven me," she mumbled. No surprise there. Sawyer wasn't ever likely to forgive her.

"What do you think?" he mumbled back.

His voice was a growl, and it should have unnerved her. Along with that steely glare he was giving her. But sadly, even now, her reaction to Sawyer was a different kind of unnerving.

The images of them naked in bed flashed through her mind. Memorable images. But with bad timing. Then and now. She had been his one-night stand.

His decision, not hers.

She'd known him for months before that one-nighter. Months of lusting after him. And when Cassidy had finally run into him at a party, they'd left together to go back to his place for that one glorious night.

"I was attracted to you," she reminded him. Still was. "That's why I slept with you, not so I could get information about the investigation you were conducting on my brother."

"Right," he grumbled. "But it was a nice perk that you got that information."

Cassidy swallowed hard. "Only by accident, because I overheard your phone conversation with your boss."

"Worked in your favor, didn't it." Not a question. He spoke it as gospel.

And it was something she couldn't argue with.

She had alerted her brother about the investigation into his possible involvement with money laundering. Not intentionally but only because she'd questioned Bennie about it. She hadn't wanted to believe he was involved in something so awful. However, Sawyer was certain that Bennie had used that info to cover his tracks so he couldn't be arrested.

Maybe he had.

But when she'd slept with Sawyer, she certainly hadn't

known that was going to happen. An investigation had been the last thing on her mind.

Sawyer pulled into the parking lot of the hospital, and he made more of those glances around before he got out and ushered her inside and to the E.R. The first sound she heard was a baby crying, and they followed that sound to an examining room, where she spotted a dark-haired man holding the baby.

Cassidy actually dropped back a step. This guy had a deputy's badge clipped to his belt, but with his desperado stubble and hard eyes, he looked more outlaw than lawman.

"Hope you have better luck with her than I have," the man said over the baby's cries. "She won't hush. Won't take her bottle, either." And he eased the baby into Sawyer's arms.

Despite everything that had just happened, Sawyer looked amused. Well, for a split second he did.

"Your wife's due any day now," Sawyer said to the man. "Better get used to it."

The deputy grumbled something Cassidy didn't catch and put the baby's bottle on the table next to Sawyer.

"This is Mason, my cousin," Sawyer told her. "And this is Cassidy O'Neal."

Mason made a sound deep in his throat that she figured was disapproval. It was possible Sawyer had spilled all about their brief affair, and even if he hadn't, she was sure her reputation preceded her. Most people thought she was a spoiled heiress. She was rich but worked plenty hard to manage the real estate investment business that her late parents had left her and her brother.

With his attention on the baby, Sawyer dropped into the chair and studied the baby's face. No doubt trying to decide if she was his. At least the baby stopped crying, and she looked up at Sawyer, examining him with the same intensity with which he was examining her.

"She's what…about a week or two old?" Sawyer asked no one in particular. "Any reports of a missing newborn?"

Mason shook his head. "None in this area. There was a newborn boy taken in San Antonio, but that was a custody dispute." He checked the time. "I'll see what's keeping Dr. Michelson. He said he'll examine Cassidy, but if she's hurt, you're to take her over to one of the E.R. docs right away," he added.

"I'm not hurt," she insisted.

"Then I'll let the doc know that," Mason answered. "Right now, he's dealing with Social Services. They're supposed to come and get the baby."

Sawyer's head whipped up, as if he might challenge that, but he didn't. Cassidy thought she might challenge it, too. She'd been in the Social Services system briefly when her parents died, but she had been sixteen. And could fend for herself. Plus, a huge inheritance had helped pave the way to her emancipation, but it cut her to the core to realize this baby could be handed over to strangers while the truth was sorted out.

And speaking of sorting, Sawyer looked to be doing just that. He took out his phone and scrolled through the numbers. Since that wasn't easy to do with the baby in his arms, Cassidy took the child, easing her into the crook of her arm. It didn't exactly feel natural since she didn't have much experience with babies, but it didn't feel wrong, either.

Not the best time for her biological clock to start ticking.

Sawyer clicked on one of the numbers, waited. "Laurie," he said when the woman obviously answered.

Cassidy felt an emotion of a different kind. A punch

of jealousy, and she would have laughed at herself for feeling it, but laughter at this point would no doubt make Sawyer think she was insane. Maybe she was, for still feeling attracted to a man who clearly hated her.

"Yeah, I'd like to catch up, too," he added a moment later, "but maybe some other time." Sawyer paused, his forehead bunching up. "Uh, did you recently have a baby?"

Unlike in the truck, Cassidy couldn't hear what the woman said, but judging from Sawyer's reaction it wasn't good. "Sorry to have bothered you," he added a moment later and ended the call.

"Well?" Cassidy asked when he didn't say anything to her.

However, all she got from Sawyer was another shoulder lift. "It's not Laurie's baby."

Which meant it wasn't Sawyer's.

"Then, who is she?" Cassidy looked down at the baby. So precious and little. She touched her finger to the baby's hand, and the little girl grabbed on to it. "And why hasn't someone reported her missing?"

"I don't know, but if she were mine," he said under his breath, "I'd definitely be missing her."

She had to do a mental double take at that. Sawyer was the ultimate bad boy, the reason she'd been attracted to him in the first place. But this was a side of him that she'd never seen, and he suddenly looked uncomfortable that he'd let her get a glimpse of it.

"Is there anyone else that you could have gotten pregnant?" she came out and asked.

"Other than Laurie or you," he said, stating the obvious. "There's one other woman. I barely knew her. It was a hookup-at-a-party kind of thing. I'm not sure how to get in touch with her."

"With your FBI resources, you should—" But she stopped. Rethought that. "You don't remember her name."

Sawyer scrubbed his hand over his face. "No. But I doubt she remembers mine, either. And if you think I'm proud of that, I'm not."

He stood, as if ready to take the baby from her, but then they heard footsteps. Clearly, they were both still on edge because Sawyer stepped protectively in front of her and the baby. But it wasn't a threat.

Well, not a real one anyway.

It was Mason.

"Just got off the phone with Gage," he said.

"Did they find Bennie?" Cassidy immediately asked.

Mason shook his head. "They're still looking. The doc's still working on the papers for Social Services, and then he'll examine you." Mason turned his attention to Sawyer. "But Gage found out the dead woman, April Warrick, was a con artist with a mile-long rap sheet."

"Any kidnapping charges on it?" Sawyer wanted to know.

"None." Mason shifted his attention to the baby. "But April gave birth about ten days ago. She had a girl. We don't know much more than that, but she was a criminal informant for the San Antonio P.D. Nate's looking into it now and should be calling you any minute."

"Nate and Gage are Mason's brothers," Sawyer explained to her, but she could tell his mind was on other things.

Mason reached for the baby. "Why don't I go ahead and take her to the hospital nursery. It could take a while for Social Services to get here."

"No," Cassidy jumped to say. It was crazy, but she wanted to keep the baby with her as long as possible.

Mason looked at Sawyer, obviously waiting for his

say in the matter, and Sawyer finally nodded. "After the doc's checked out Cassidy, I'll bring the baby to the nursery and then head to the sheriff's office so we can write our reports."

Mason didn't question that, though it probably did seem strange to him. He made a sound that could have meant anything and strolled away.

"You can't keep her, you know," Sawyer said, standing. He went to her, looking down at the baby, and he touched the little girl's cheek with this finger.

The corner of the baby's mouth lifted as if she was smiling.

And that caused Cassidy to smile, too. Well, for a few seconds anyway, and then reality hit her.

"If April was her mother, then her next of kin is her father." She hated to say it aloud, but she figured Sawyer was thinking it, too. "What if her father's the other kidnapper?"

"It's possible," Sawyer readily admitted. "That's why we need to catch him and then get the results from the DNA and blood tests. We might be able to exclude him on the blood test alone."

Yes, but it wouldn't solve her other problem of finding Bennie. If the kidnapper had murdered his own lover, the mother of his child, and used that child in some kind of kidnapping scheme, then she wanted her brother far away from this monster.

Sawyer's phone buzzed, and because he was so close to her, she saw the name on the phone screen.

Nate Ryland.

His cousin and the cop from SAPD that Mason had mentioned. Sawyer stepped away from her, but he did put the call on speaker.

"Mason said you wanted some info on April Warrick,"

Nate started. "Well, that's her body you found in Silver Creek. Grayson sent me a photo, and I was able to confirm it with Doug Franklin, the detective who used her as a criminal informant."

Cassidy was glad the baby was too young to understand the news they'd just gotten.

"Did April really have a baby?" Sawyer asked.

"Yeah. A girl, but I can't confirm if it's the baby that the kidnappers had. Still working on that. But we do have a lead. Doug said last year April was involved with a real hothead. A guy named Willy Malloy."

Sawyer took a notepad from his pocket and wrote down the name. "I want to talk to him."

"Figured you would. I'll track him down and get him out to Silver Creek so Grayson and you can question him." Nate paused. "There's someone else you'll want to talk to. A couple of months ago, April was ordered to see a court-appointed therapist, Dr. Diane Blackwell. She's already called here looking for April, and I told her to get in touch with you."

A therapist could definitely give them some info. If she'd talk, that is. Cassidy hoped she didn't play the client-confidentiality card, especially now that her client was dead.

"There's more," Nate said a moment later. "Doug said April hadn't mentioned Willy in months, that she'd been seeing some rich guy, and that April was worried that the guy might be up to no good."

"You got a name?" Sawyer asked.

"Yeah. It's a name you're not going to like. Doug said it was Bennie O'Neal."

Cassidy wasn't able to bite back her gasp. *No.* This couldn't be happening. But Sawyer only tossed her an I-told-you-so look.

"The detective said if you want to find April's killer," Nate added, "then start with Bennie—that judging from the way April talked bad about him, he's the one who probably murdered her."

Chapter Five

Sawyer finished up the call with his brother, Josh, and gave him both an apology for having to leave the reception early and well-wishes since Josh was about to leave on his honeymoon with his new bride. Even though Josh had asked about the kidnapping, Sawyer kept the details brief. No need to trouble his brother with a case that didn't make sense anyway.

When he ended the call, he glanced up to check on Cassidy. Sawyer had no idea what to do about her. Obviously waiting, she was pacing the hall of the Silver Creek sheriff's office. The trouble was, it might be a long time before they heard anything from the kidnappers.

If there were indeed kidnappers.

It was possible this was all some kind of elaborate scheme concocted by Bennie to get his sister's money under the guise of a ransom. That part of the twisted plan actually made sense, but not much else did.

Like why had April been murdered?

And why had the kidnappers demanded a photo of Sawyer holding a stranger's baby? A baby who may or may not belong to April.

One thing was certain—the little girl wasn't Laurie's and his. Sawyer wanted to be relieved about that, but there was a flip side to this coin. At least if he was her father, he could have decided her fate. He could have made sure she was in a good place where she'd be safe—with him. As it was now, the baby would become a ward of the state, and that was, sadly, a best-case scenario.

There was a birth father out there. And judging from April's rap sheet, that father might be scum.

Either her ex-boyfriend Willy Malloy.

Or Bennie.

Sawyer didn't want either man to have a claim on the newborn and didn't want the baby to be placed in their care. Of course, he might not have to worry about that if it turned out that April wasn't the baby's mother. And if she wasn't, he really needed to remember the name of the woman he'd met at the bar.

Because if that woman was the mother, then it meant the baby could possibly be his after all since they'd had a one-night stand.

Yeah, this was a tangled mess, all right.

Cassidy paced by the office door again, and Sawyer saw her check the clock on the wall next to the sheriff's desk. It was going on 6:00 p.m.

"The kidnappers should have called by now," she grumbled. "Maybe I should check and make sure the calls to my house are routed here."

"If a call comes in there, you'll get it here," he assured her.

He'd made the arrangements for that himself. Ditto for getting her a replacement cell phone with the same number, and he'd had it delivered to the office so the kidnappers could contact her. She had a death grip on the phone now, and other than some emails having to do with her family business, there had been no communication from anyone.

Especially not from Bennie.

She huffed, pushed her hair from her face. "Maybe I should just go home and wait for the call."

He gave her a flat look to let her know that wasn't going to happen. Not without him anyway. "Should I remind you one more time that you were kidnapped, too? Those thugs might try to take you again, and the safest place you can be is here with me."

Sawyer hoped that was true anyway.

He didn't have time to add to his argument because his phone rang, and he saw Mason's name on the screen.

"There's been a snafu with Social Services," Mason said, "and they want to know if we can keep the baby overnight. It's either that, or she can be admitted to the hospital."

Even though Cassidy probably couldn't have heard what he said, she was studying Sawyer's face and obviously saw the concern in his expression.

"No hospital," Sawyer insisted. "Go ahead and take the baby to the ranch. Cassidy and I will be there soon to pick her up and take her to my place."

He ended the call, knowing that she'd want an explanation about several things. "It's either the hospital or my house for the baby," he said. "I figured she's already been through enough. And besides, there are plenty of us at the ranch to help take care of her."

"Including me?" Cassidy asked with a boatload of skepticism.

And here was the part she was *not* going to like. Heck, Sawyer didn't like it much, either. "You need to be in protective custody. So does the baby. Because the kidnappers could come after either of you again."

Cassidy's mouth trembled a little. Not enough to stop her from arguing though. "But your family's ranch? I won't be welcome there."

"You won't be turned away. Besides, there's a lot of baby stuff already out there."

In addition, there were plenty of ranch hands who could provide extra security. To get that kind of security at the hospital, he'd have to tie up several of Grayson's deputies. They were already busy enough with a murder investigation, the kidnappings and the search for Bennie.

"We'd be in the same house with all your cousins?" Cassidy asked, nibbling on her lip.

"No. There are a lot of houses on the grounds. Including mine. It's on the back part of the property. It used to be my parents' house before their divorce."

Definitely a no-frills kind of place, but it suited Sawyer, and it would have to suit Cassidy, too, since he wasn't giving her another option.

She still didn't look convinced, but she didn't have time to continue the argument. The bell on the front door jangled, and Sawyer pulled Cassidy into the office just in case there was a problem.

And there might be.

The man who stepped into the sheriff's office had trouble written all over him. From his greasy black hair, prison tattoos on his neck and dingy gray muscle shirt.

"I'm Willy Malloy," he told the woman at the reception desk, who was Deputy Bree Ryland—his cousin's wife. And as she stood, she slid her hand over the butt of her gun.

If Willy was intimidated by that, he didn't show it. The man's gaze landed on Sawyer. "Are you Agent Ryland?"

Sawyer nodded and gave him back the badass stare that the man was giving him. "Wait here," he told Cassidy, and Sawyer walked a few steps closer to the man.

"You gonna pay me back for gas?" Willy asked, propping his hands on his bony hips. "Because it was a long drive all the way out here, and I'm not made of money."

"Didn't figure you'd mind the drive since this visit is about April, your ex."

Judging from the surprised look in his eyes, that got Willy's attention. "She's not my ex. She's still my girlfriend, and I've been looking for her for months now. You know where she is?"

Oh, man.

Willy hadn't heard about the murder, or else he was pretending not to have heard. In case it wasn't an act, Sawyer decided to do this fast and hard.

"April's dead. Did you kill her?" Sawyer asked, and he studied Willy's body language and expression.

Sawyer expected the man to curse or howl his innocence, but he just stood there, his mouth open, staring at Sawyer. "Is this some kind of bad joke?"

"No. Someone murdered her earlier today. Was it you?"

Willy put his hands on each side of his head, and blowing out some loud breaths, he practically fell back against the wall. "Murdered," he repeated. "Who the hell did that to her?"

"I asked you first," Sawyer fired back.

"Well, it sure as heck wasn't me. I love her. I wouldn't have killed her."

Sawyer looked down at the notes he'd been reading. "According to your rap sheet, you were arrested for assaulting her not once but twice. Doesn't sound like love to me."

"I slapped her around, yeah. And she deserved it. That woman's got a smart mouth on her." Willy stopped, shook his head. "*Had* a smart mouth," he corrected, groaning. "She sure as heck didn't deserve to die. How'd it happen? How was she killed?"

"We're still trying to determine that." It was a lie. She'd been shot point-blank in the head, but Sawyer kept that detail to himself. Best not to give a suspect too much information because Willy could use it to concoct an alibi.

Despite his warning, Cassidy stepped into the hall. "My brother's Bennie O'Neal. Do you have any idea where he is?"

Willy's eyes instantly narrowed. "Bennie O'Neal," he repeated like profanity. "He's the no-good louse that April was cheating on me with. I warned both of them that it wouldn't be a pretty sight if they kept it up."

"So you threatened them," Sawyer concluded. He was detecting a pattern here, and he got in front of Cassidy to stop her from moving closer to the man.

No more narrowed eyes. Willy no doubt realized that wasn't the right thing to say to a lawman, especially since he was now a murder suspect. "I got a right to protect what's mine, and April was mine."

Sawyer doubted that, and he asked a necessary question he didn't really want to ask this thug. "What about the baby?"

Willy's mouth tightened. "What about it?"

"You did know that April was pregnant?" Sawyer prompted when Willy didn't add more.

"I knew." And that's all he said for several moments. "April said the kid was mine. Wouldn't believe her without one of those paternity tests. April's not real good on telling the truth. So, she said she'd do the test they do on unborn babies. But if she had it done, she never showed me the results. Probably because the kid wasn't mine."

Or maybe because April hadn't wanted Willy in her and the baby's life.

Sawyer tipped his head to Bree and then the supply

cabinet. "We'll need to verify what April didn't tell him." And he didn't especially want to leave Cassidy alone with this piece of work while that happened.

"I'll get a DNA swab kit," Bree volunteered, moving out of the reception area and down the hall.

"Now, wait a minute," Willy challenged. Bree didn't stop. She continued toward the supply cabinet. "If April's dead, so is the kid, right?"

"No." Except Sawyer didn't know if that was true or not. He was assuming the baby that the kidnappers gave Cassidy was April's child. But maybe she wasn't.

"Are you saying she had the kid already?" Willy pressed.

Sawyer settled for a nod.

Willy cursed and his hands went back on his hips. "Then, the kid's not mine. Can't be. April and me have what you call an on-again, off-again kind of relationship. Nine months ago, we were definitely off."

"Then, how the devil do you still consider her your girlfriend?"

"Easy. We got back together about six months ago. Things stayed hot and heavy for about a month, and then she lit out again after telling me she was pregnant."

Willy's gaze shot to Cassidy. "And I figured that's when she went to your slimeball brother." More cursing. "If that was his kid, if April got knocked up by another man, then she deserved to die."

And that just spelled out Willy's motive for murder.

"You killed her," Cassidy concluded. "Did you do something to my brother, too?" That time, Sawyer wasn't able to hold her back, so he followed her to the front of the building.

"I didn't kill nobody," Willy snapped. "But if I was

planning to do something stupid like that, your brother would have been on my list."

Willy just kept digging that hole deeper and deeper.

Sawyer and Bree exchanged a glance as she walked past him with the DNA kit. "Want me to move him to an interview room and take his statement?" Bree asked, and Sawyer nodded.

"Statement?" Willy howled. "I don't have time for that kind of nonsense."

"You'll make time. If not, I'll just arrest you now and charge you with murder," Sawyer warned him.

That obviously didn't please Willy. It didn't please Sawyer, either. Even though he wanted this idiot off the street, it wasn't a good time to make an arrest.

Not with so many details to work out.

Heck, Willy might even have an airtight alibi. A real honest-to-goodness one. But if Willy was the kidnapper and had helped orchestrate all of this, then maybe he was stupid enough to have left evidence behind.

Bree handed Willy the swab from the kit. "You can do it yourself, or Agent Ryland here and I can do it for you."

Willy shot all three of them glares, but he rubbed the swab on the inside of his mouth past his chipped, yellow teeth, and he dropped it back into the plastic bag.

"Let's go to an interview room," Bree insisted, sealing the bag and motioning for Willy to follow her. He did, after mumbling more profanity, but then he stopped when the woman approaching the door caught everyone's attention.

The tall, thin brunette stepped into the sheriff's office. She closed her umbrella, set it by the door and looked around at all of them. She was dressed to the nines, all right. A pale gray suit and mile-high heels. Expensive, no doubt. Ditto for the chunky diamond wedding ring.

Her expression was pleasant enough until it landed on Willy. "I see you've already brought him in," she said. "I'm Dr. Diane Blackwell. I was April's therapist. I understand you'd like to talk to me?"

"I would," Sawyer confirmed. He studied her a moment. "You look pretty young for a shrink." He doubted she was even thirty yet.

The corner of her mouth lifted a fraction. "Thank you, I think. I'll accept that as a compliment and not a concern that I might be too young to be an effective therapist. Trust me, I'm very good at my job."

Sawyer considered that for a moment and decided to do a background check on her just to see how good she was. "I'm Agent Sawyer Ryland," he said, making the introductions. "And this is Deputy Bree Ryland and Cassidy O'Neal."

The doctor's gaze lingered a moment on Cassidy, maybe wondering what she had to do with all of this, but she didn't ask any questions.

"The doc's nothing more than a quack shrink," Willy snarled. "The judge made April see her once a week, and April was scared to death of her."

Until Willy had added that last part, Sawyer had been ready to stop this little confrontation, but maybe he could learn something that would help the investigation.

Especially since Diane didn't jump to argue with Willy.

"Last time April and me talked," Willy went on, "she said she thought this quack was messing with her mind."

Diane dismissed that with a cool glance at Willy. "April was a troubled woman, and she was terrified of you."

"So says you, and now that April's dead, I got no way of proving different."

"That's right." Diane spared him another frosty glance

with her cool green eyes before fastening her attention on Sawyer. "I'll try to answer any questions you have. I want to help you catch April's killer." And judging from the quick glare she gave Willy, she thought he was that killer.

"Come on," Bree instructed Willy, and she led him to the first interview room.

"Don't believe a word that quack says," Willy warned them. "And if she tries to pin this murder on me, she'll be sorry."

Other than a single soft sigh, Diane had no reaction to Willy's threat. Bree, however, did. She put her hand on Willy's shoulder and practically shoved him into the interview room. Sawyer waited a moment to see if Bree needed some help, but obviously she didn't. Bree might be on the petite side, but she had a tough lawman's attitude and a whole lot of Ryland muscle to back her up if the attitude didn't work.

"Tell me where you were this morning," Bree ordered Willy.

While the doctor made her way toward them, Sawyer listened in on Willy's answer.

"At home sleeping in. And before you ask, no one can verify that 'cause I live all by my lonesome. That still don't make me a killer."

No, but it made him a violent man with no alibi and a strong motive for murdering April.

Sawyer stepped into Grayson's office with Cassidy, and Diane followed him.

"We've met," Diane said to Cassidy and extended her hand for Cassidy to shake. "At a fund-raiser last year in San Antonio. I don't expect you to remember, but someone introduced me to you and your brother."

Judging from Cassidy's reaction, that wasn't much of

a surprise. Probably because she attended a lot of functions like that.

"Now, back to April," Diane went on. "Like I said earlier, she was a troubled woman. I'd be happy to help you in any way that I can."

So, her offer of help was one possible roadblock removed, and Sawyer didn't waste any time. "When's the last time you saw her?"

"Two weeks ago for our regular counseling session. When she didn't show for her appointment yesterday, I had to report it to the judge. It's part of her parole agreement." She opened her mouth, no doubt to ask some questions of her own, but Sawyer went first.

"April was still pregnant two weeks ago?"

Diane nodded. Then she gasped, touching her perfectly manicured peach fingernails to her color-coordinated mouth. "Oh, God. Please tell me her killer didn't hurt the baby, too."

"I don't think so. We're trying to determine if it's her baby that we found. Any idea if April was involved in something illegal? Like kidnapping maybe?"

Diane's eyes suddenly weren't so cool. There was concern in them. "She didn't say anything about breaking the law again. Why, is that what happened?"

"I'm not sure." And that wasn't a lie. Sawyer didn't know. Just because the woman associated with thugs and had a criminal record, it didn't mean she was up to no good this time around. She could have just been in the wrong place at the wrong time.

"Did April say anything about my brother, Bennie?" Cassidy blurted out.

"Only that she was seeing him. Why?" Diane asked. "Does your brother have something to do with her murder?"

Sawyer hoped not. For Cassidy's sake. "When you last saw April," Sawyer continued, "did she seem unnerved about anything?"

Diane drew in a weary breath. "Only Willy. She was trying to hide from him, but she was worried that he was going to track her down at one of our appointments. That's why we changed the dates several times, and then I finally just moved our sessions to my home. She was terrified that Willy would do something to make her lose the baby."

Because Willy thought the baby wasn't his. "Why did Willy think April was afraid of you?"

Diane shrugged, then huffed. "Probably because the counseling sessions with April were court-appointed. He's a career criminal with a violent streak. I suspect he doesn't trust anyone or anything associated with the law."

That made sense. In a way. Still, Sawyer had to wonder if that was all there was to it.

Diane opened her purse, extracted a business card and handed it to Sawyer. "Call me if you hear anything. Or if I can help. As I said, I'm anxious to help catch whoever did this to April."

She turned to leave, but Sawyer stopped her. "You didn't ask how April was murdered," he said.

Diane blinked, and for just a split second there seemed to be some panic in her eyes. "I assumed you'd tell me if you could. Police hold that type of information back sometimes."

"Sometimes," he repeated, continuing to watch her and continuing to give her a suspicious once-over.

No crack in the composure this time. Diane issued a crisp goodbye and walked out, her pricey heels clicking on the tile floor.

"You don't trust her?" Cassidy asked.

"The jury's still out on that." He wasn't about to distrust her only because of the things Willy had said. Because Sawyer definitely didn't trust April's tattooed ex.

Sawyer glanced at the interview room. "I'll call one of the other deputies, and once he's here, we can leave for the ranch."

Where maybe Cassidy would get some rest. She looked ready to fall on her face. Sawyer took out his phone, but Cassidy's rang before he had a chance to make the call. There was no name or number. The caller had blocked the info.

He pushed the button to answer it and put the call on speaker so Cassidy could hear.

"Ms. O'Neal?" the caller said in a mechanical voice. It was obviously being filtered through some kind of voice-alteration device. "We're the people who have your brother."

"Is Bennie all right?" she immediately asked.

"For now. You were late bringing that photo, and it's going to cost you. Or better yet, it'll cost your brother—"

"No, please. Don't hurt him."

"We won't if you do exactly as we say. Tomorrow morning at ten, you and Agent Sawyer Ryland are to deliver the money to us. We'll be calling back with details of the location."

"We need to speak to Bennie," Sawyer insisted. "To make sure he's still alive."

"Tomorrow you'll get the chance to talk to him and see him if you follow the rules. A half-million dollars, and only the two of you will come for the exchange. Mess it up again, Ms. O'Neal, and you'll get your brother killed."

"Please, let me talk to him," Cassidy begged.

But she was talking to the air because the kidnapper had already hung up.

Chapter Six

Cassidy stepped into the sprawling ranch house just ahead of Sawyer, and the first thing she heard were the sounds of children.

Lots of them.

"This way," Sawyer said, and he led her down a corridor and to a massive playroom, where she spotted a man and three kids. Two dark-haired toddler girls and a little boy about the same age. The room was filled with all sorts of toys, books and games, and there were several playpens and cribs positioned against the walls.

The man was stretched out on the floor while the children ran circles around him. Occasionally, the man would reach up and goose out of them on their bellies. They were clearly enjoying the game because they howled with laughter.

Despite the happy scene, Cassidy's heart dropped when she didn't immediately see the baby, but then she spotted her in a wicker basket on the table next to the man. She was sound asleep, though Cassidy didn't know how she managed it with all the noise.

"This is Gage," Sawyer said, tipping his head to the goosing man. "Another cousin. He's a Silver Creek deputy, and the father of that one." He pointed to the boy.

"His name is Luke. And the other two are Bree and Kade's twins, Leah and Mia. Folks, this is Cassidy."

Gage sat up, flashing a smile that was familiar. Apparently, it was a Ryland trait, because she'd seen the same smile on Sawyer. She'd called it a bedroom smile because that's exactly where it had caused her and Sawyer to land.

Cassidy pushed aside the heat that came with those memories and wondered when she was ever going to forget them. Maybe once she managed to put some space between Sawyer and her, but heaven knows when that was going to happen. She just seemed to keep getting in deeper and deeper with him.

Now they were supposed to do a ransom drop together.

That definitely wouldn't give her any space.

"I see you got babysitting duty," Sawyer remarked to Gage.

"Yeah, everybody's tied up with the investigation and other stuff. The baby's already had her bottle and a diaper change. Much easier changing her than my boy." He hitched his thumb toward his son. "Luke thinks diaper time is practice for hosing me down."

The little boy paused, only to grin at his dad, and continued the game.

"Any breaks in the case?" Gage asked.

"None," Sawyer answered. "Ransom drop's supposed to be tomorrow. The kidnappers will give us the location and details then."

Cassidy needed to focus on the conversation, but it was hard to do that when the three children started running around her. Apparently, they were resuming their game, and she was to be the new gooser. She truly sucked at it because on her first attempt, she nearly poked one of the little girls in the eye.

"And what about her?" Gage asked, glancing at the baby.

Sawyer lifted his shoulder. "The doctor took a sample of her DNA and blood. We could know soon if the dead woman was her mother."

And they'd also know who the father was.

She didn't miss the way Gage volleyed glances between Sawyer and the baby. "You think she's yours?"

Sawyer didn't jump to answer. "Maybe. I've ruled out one woman, but there was someone else. Just a one-nighter, and I haven't been able to track her down."

A one-nighter. Like Cassidy. It shouldn't have stung, but it did, and it made her wonder just how many women that smile and those hot looks had seduced.

She really didn't want to know.

"Just give me a call if you need any help," Gage offered, and he motioned toward the diaper bag next to the baby. "I think you'll find everything you need in there." He paused though, glanced at both Sawyer and her. "You two sure you're up to this? A newborn's a lot of work."

"We're up to it," she heard herself say, though Cassidy had no idea if they truly were. All she knew was she didn't want the baby to have to spend the night in the hospital and she didn't want to have to stay the night at the Ryland ranch with all of Sawyer's kin around. It would be bad enough with just the two of them at his place.

Three of them, she corrected.

Having the baby around would make her stay with Sawyer seem less, well, intimate. Not that he had any notion of intimacy happening between them.

Sawyer looped the diaper bag over his shoulder and

reached for the baby, but the sounds of footsteps and voices stopped him.

Even though she figured the ranch was safe, Cassidy still went on alert. However, it was a false alarm because Mason and a very pregnant brunette came into the room. They were kissing and seemingly ignoring the kids trailing along with them.

The woman broke the kiss with Mason. His wife, no doubt. And her face flushed a little when she saw Cassidy and Sawyer. Smiling, she made her way to Cassidy and offered her hand.

"I'm Abbie Ryland. I hope Gage welcomed you to our *quiet* home."

Cassidy nodded and watched the children stream in.

Abbie laughed at her slack-jawed reaction. Mason mumbled something about them having their own baseball team. But there seemed to be a lot more than just nine of them.

"That's Robbie," Abbie said, pointing to a little boy who was about three. "He's Dade and Kayla's son." She looked around the room, spotted a toddler with loose brown curls and enormous gray eyes. "And that's their daughter, Meggie. Be careful, she bites."

Cassidy felt more than a little foolish when she dropped back a step. The little girl looked like an angel. But she did have teeth.

Mason scooped up one of the boys and tossed him over his shoulder. "This is Grayson's boy, Chet. The rest are Nate and Darcy's brood. Kimmie, Noah and Bella."

Kimmie was a red-haired girl about four. Noah appeared to be about the same age, and the other girl, Bella, looked to be around two.

"How do you keep them all straight?" Cassidy asked, and even though Abbie chuckled, it wasn't exactly a joke.

The red-haired girl made a beeline for Abbie. "Hello, Max." She got on her tiptoes to kiss Abbie's very pregnant belly. "When can he come out and play with us?"

"Hopefully, very soon," Abbie said at the same moment Mason said, "Not soon enough."

The little girl made a *hmm*ing sound. "You sure Max knows how to get out of there?"

Gage sputtered out a cough, laughing. Sawyer covered a laugh, too. Mason just looked his normal ornery self. Well, until he patted his wife's belly, and some of the orneriness vanished.

"Don't worry," Mason told Kimmie, ruffling her curly red hair. "The doctor will give Max directions."

That answer seemed to satisfy Kimmie, and her attention landed on the baby. "Aw, she's still sleeping. When's she gonna wake up?"

"Pretty soon if you don't lower your voice," Gage teased.

But Kimmie gave her uncle a play punch on the arm and peered into the basket again. "Can we name her Emma?"

"Isn't that your doll's name?" Abbie asked.

"Yeah, but she could share it. It's a good name, and I can spell it already." Kimmie did exactly that and looked at Sawyer, obviously waiting for his approval.

He finally nodded. "All right. We'll call her Emma until we find out what her real name is. But you know that she can't stay with us, right?"

That sent some yelps and rumbles of disapproval from the three girls and Noah. It was amazing that with all these playmates, they would want more.

They were family.

And that hit Cassidy hard, too.

It had only been Bennie and her for the past fourteen

years. Their parents had been killed when she was only a teenager. Bennie had been just ten. Hard to make a family under those circumstances, but Cassidy had tried.

For all the good it had done her.

Now Bennie's life was on the line, and she might not even be able to save him.

The touch on her arm nearly caused her to gasp, until Cassidy realized it was Sawyer. "Ready to go?" he asked over the chatter of the children. She wasn't sure when he'd done it, but he had the baby, basket and all, tucked beneath his arm.

She nodded and managed to say, "It was nice to meet you," to the Ryland clan.

"Social Services will probably be by your place first thing in the morning," Mason told them. "You're sure you don't want her to stay with one of the nannies tonight?"

Sawyer shook his head. "The nannies and the rest of you have your hands full. But I'll need a vehicle with an infant seat. Is there one out back?"

"Several," Gage verified. "The keys are in the mudroom. Pick one with a pink key chain." He shrugged when Sawyer and Cassidy stared at him. "Hey, with this many kids, you gotta keep things simple."

Sawyer smiled, shook his head and brushed a kiss on Abbie's cheek before he ushered Cassidy out of the chaos and back into the hall.

"You okay?" he asked her.

She nodded, but it was a lie. "I'm worried about tomorrow." First, though, she had to get through the night.

"Yeah." And that's all he said. It seemed to be enough, especially considering she'd just witnessed how important family was to him. Still, Bennie wasn't just her family. He was more like her own son.

When they reached the mudroom off the kitchen, she

spotted the key rack near the door, and there were indeed two sets with a pink plastic key ring. Sawyer plucked one, opened the door and clicked the keypad. The lights on a dark green SUV came on, and they hurried to it. It had finally stopped raining, but there was a cool mist in the air, so it was best to get the baby inside.

She watched as Sawyer moved the baby from the basket to the car seat. "I've gotten good at this," he mumbled when he caught her staring at him.

Yes, he had, and somehow it didn't hurt his bad-boy image.

Sawyer took a narrow dirt-and-gravel road that led away from the main house. They passed several other houses, some barns and plenty of pasture before she spotted his place. He hadn't exaggerated when he'd said it was on the back part of the ranch. Sawyer had to go through a cattle gate to reach the one-story white limestone house.

"The place didn't used to be part of the Silver Creek Ranch," he told her. "But after I moved back two years ago, my uncle Boone repositioned the fence to include my house."

"Does that mean there's a security system?" she asked.

He nodded. "Both inside and out. There are sensors on the fence that'll trigger an alarm if anyone tries to get to the house by cutting through the woods."

Good. She wanted all the precautions they could take, especially since the baby was with them.

Sawyer didn't waste any time getting them into the house, but the movement woke the baby. The moment he set the basket on the kitchen table, she started to cry. Not a loud wail but rather soft, kittenlike sounds. Still, it was more than enough to get their attention. Cassidy was ready to scoop her up, but the baby closed her eyes and went back to sleep.

Cassidy's shoulders dropped. She was far from a pro at baby holding, but it would have given her suddenly restless hands and mind something to do.

Other than worry about her brother.

Sawyer used the keypad by the door to set the security system, and he tipped his head to the fridge. "Help yourself. I know you must be hungry."

She wasn't. Her stomach was still in knots.

"This way to the guest room." He picked up the basket, and they moved toward the side of the house. "I'm here," he said, pointing to one bedroom. "You're there."

There in this case was directly across the hall from his room. That sent some heat running through her, but the heat cooled when she looked at the baby.

"What about Emma?" she asked.

He lifted an eyebrow, probably at the easy use of the name that Kimmie had given her, but it was better than just calling her "the baby."

"I'll put the basket on the cedar chest at the foot of my bed. I'm guessing she…Emma," he corrected, "will wake up at least a couple of times. So, if you want to get some rest, you'll have to close the door."

"I'll be fine," Cassidy settled for saying. And she'd keep the door open. Not just so she could hear and maybe help with the baby but because she wanted to know if someone tried to break in.

Sawyer studied her a moment, frowned. "You don't look fine. Your nerves are showing."

Until he said that, Cassidy had thought she'd been keeping those nerves at bay. Well, almost. But his words brought them right back to the surface. "I'm worried about Bennie. About tomorrow." Her voice cracked, causing her to silently curse.

Tears and a shaky voice weren't going to help, but she couldn't seem to stop, either.

"It's part of the adrenaline crash," Sawyer supplied, and he eased the basket onto the cedar chest. "A hot shower might help."

She nodded but didn't move. "I have the ransom money waiting at the bank, but maybe I should have brought it here. Just in case they give us a short window for delivering the money."

He walked to her, huffed. "*Us,* again? I'm going to try hard to make sure there is no *us* for the money drop."

"That didn't work out so well last time." She'd meant to sound tough, but her quivery voice told a different story.

"It'll work this time," he said with complete assurance. It was probably wishful thinking at best and a lie at worst, but Cassidy decided to accept it.

For now anyway.

He reached out as if he might touch her but then drew back his hand. "Probably not a good idea," he mumbled.

It wasn't.

Still, that didn't stop him from running his hand down her arm. It was a friendly soothing gesture, and she was surprised how much it helped with those unsteady nerves.

"I'll take that shower now," she said. But Cassidy didn't move.

She stood there, her gaze connected with Sawyer's, and his hand on her arm. A dozen things went through her mind, including an attempt to convince him once more that she hadn't slept with him to get info about his investigation into her brother. However, she doubted she'd ever convince him of that.

Then Cassidy saw it. The fire burning in his sizzling blue eyes. And she also saw that he was as disgusted with it as he was with her. But despite the fierce battle in those eyes, she also saw it was a battle he was losing.

Oh, no.

He couldn't lose. Not with stakes this high. And Cassidy was certain she had no willpower to resist anything he doled out.

Cursing her, then cursing himself, Sawyer leaned in and brushed his mouth over hers. She expected it to stop there, that just the brief touch would bring him back to his senses, but it didn't. After more profanity, he caught her around the waist, yanked her to him and kissed her.

Really kissed her.

There was no way this was just to comfort her. Good thing, too, because it was anything but comforting. Sawyer's mouth moved over hers, fanning that fire even hotter when he deepened the kiss.

Yes! went through her head.

Along with all the sensations going through her body.

The heat. The pleasure. Especially that. The taste of him. Soon, very soon, Cassidy was doing some kiss-deepening of her own. Touching, too, with her body pressed against his. There was just one problem—a mere kiss wasn't going to get her close enough to him to satisfy the ache he'd already built inside her.

Sawyer pulled back so fast that Cassidy had to catch onto him to stop herself from falling. "Sorry," she mumbled at the same time he cursed himself again.

"You should take that shower," he snapped.

And this time she not only agreed, she turned to go into the guest room. However, she only made it a step before Sawyer's phone rang. The sound shot through the room, and despite Emma sleeping through all the kids' noise at the main house, the phone woke her and she began to cry.

Cassidy moved past Sawyer to scoop up the baby. Not that she knew what she was doing, but Cassidy tried rocking her while she also tried to listen in on Sawyer's conversation. Thankfully, he made it easier for her by putting it on speaker. The moment she heard the caller's voice, she knew it was Grayson.

Which meant this could be news about Bennie.

"We got the blood test results," Grayson said, and it took her a moment to realize this call was about Emma not her brother. "The lab can't tell paternity from blood type, but they can rule people out. Like Willy, for example. No way could he have fathered the baby."

"But?" Sawyer asked when Grayson didn't continue.

"But we can't eliminate April as the baby's mother. And we can't rule you out, Sawyer. The baby could be yours."

Chapter Seven

Sawyer sipped his coffee and tried to work. But what he ended up doing was studying the baby.

Again.

Something he'd been doing most of his waking hours. She was in her basket, sleeping after her 6:00 a.m. bottle, and even though he'd put her on her side as his cousins had instructed him to do, he still had a pretty good angle of her face.

Was she really his daughter?

He didn't have an answer for that yet, but he hoped to have one soon. It had taken several emails and phone calls before he had been able to figure out the name of the woman he'd slept with nearly a year ago.

Monica Barnes.

He wasn't proud of himself for not being able to recall that, not proud of having one-night stands, either, but now that he knew her name, he had gotten her number and tried to talk to her. There had been no answer, but Sawyer had left her a voice mail saying she needed to contact him ASAP. He'd also sent her an email.

So, soon, he should know if Emma was his.

Sawyer heard the hurried footsteps in the hall, and several moments later Cassidy came into the kitchen. She was wearing a pair of jeans and a top that one of his cousins had sent over for her. The clothes didn't fit her that well, and with her bedroom hair, she definitely didn't look her usual polished and pampered self.

"Anything from the kidnappers?" she immediately asked.

But Sawyer had to shake his head. "It's early. They'll call."

Her nerves were showing again, but this time Sawyer didn't go to her. That kiss the night before had been a huge mistake, and the way to make sure it didn't happen again was for him to keep his distance.

Not easy to do under the same roof.

And especially since his body was still attracted to her. Sawyer mentally told that part of his body to take a hike. His life was already complicated enough without adding Cassidy to the mix.

Cassidy walked closer to the baby and peered down into the basket. It hadn't been that long since she'd last seen her because Cassidy had given Emma her 2:00 a.m. bottle. Sawyer wasn't sure if he should be surprised by that or just confused. Because for a few brief moments, it felt just a little too right having both Cassidy and Emma in his kitchen.

Sawyer's computer dinged to indicate he had an email just as Cassidy helped herself to a cup of coffee. She snapped toward the screen, obviously hoping for news about her brother, but it was news of a different kind.

"Gage is helping me look for Monica Barnes," he said, reading through the message his cousin had just sent him. "That's the woman I met at a party last year."

"Oh." And that's all Cassidy said while she took a long sip of her coffee. "The woman who may be Emma's mom."

Sawyer settled for a shrug. If Monica was indeed Emma's mom, then that meant he was almost certainly

Emma's dad. It would explain why the kidnappers had wanted a photo of him holding the baby. However, it wouldn't explain what they'd planned to do with the picture.

Or the baby.

Unless they'd planned to blackmail Monica and him in some way. Monica had told him she wasn't married, and she hadn't worn a ring, but maybe there was some other reason she would want to hide a pregnancy.

"Did you find this woman?" Cassidy asked.

Sawyer finished reading the message and groaned softly. "Gage managed to track down her former boss. Monica quit her job about five months ago, and the guy hasn't heard from her since."

Her forehead bunched up. "Was she pregnant?"

Sawyer had to shake his head. "If she was, she didn't say anything about it to her boss." He paused. "But if she was carrying my child, why wouldn't she have just called and told me?"

Cassidy made a sound to indicate the answer was obvious. "She probably figured a bad boy like you wouldn't be the diaper-changing type. Sorry," she added in a mumble. "That wasn't a nice thing for me to say."

But it was true. Unlike his brother, Sawyer had never wanted marriage and kids. Never wanted the kind of life that could be shattered by a bad divorce. Like his parents'. But he darn sure wouldn't have turned his back on his own child.

The way his mother had.

Yeah, this was digging at some old wounds, but those wounds would never allow him to step away from parenthood, even in a situation like this.

"So, what will you do? How will you find Monica?" Cassidy asked.

"I'll keep searching for her. In the meantime, the baby's DNA is already at the lab, so finding Monica might not even be necessary. Since April and Emma have the same blood type, she might be her biological mother."

Which would leave them to find out the father's identity. Because Sawyer was positive he'd never been with April.

"Want some breakfast?" Sawyer asked, though Cassidy didn't have time to answer him because his phone vibrated.

He'd turned the ringer off so that it wouldn't wake the baby, but the phone rattling on the wood table did it anyway. She started to fuss, and Cassidy put her coffee aside and picked her up while Sawyer took the call from Mason. Since Mason's wife was due any day now, Sawyer expected this to be *the* call, saying they were headed to the hospital.

It wasn't.

"We might have a problem," Mason said. "Something or someone tripped the security sensor on the fence gate at the back of the property."

That instantly put a knot in his gut. "The fence near my house?"

"Yeah." There was a lot of concern in Mason's one-word response.

The fence was a recent addition. It had been added to block off an old trail that coiled around that part of the ranch. Sometimes the hands used it to get to livestock that had broken fence or to drive to some of the better hunting spots.

But Sawyer figured they weren't that lucky.

Especially since it hadn't been that long since someone had used that very trail to launch an attack on his brother and his wife. That's the reason the fence had been put up in the first place.

"It could be nothing," Mason added, "but as soon as I get a visual on one of the security cameras, I'll let you know."

Sawyer thanked him, ended the call and shoved his phone into his pocket. In the same motion, he slapped off the lights so it wouldn't be easy for anyone to spot them in the house. He also took his gun from the top of the fridge and hurried to the window over the kitchen sink. That would give him the best view of the trail and the fence.

The sun was just starting to peek over the horizon, but it was still dark enough that he couldn't see much. It didn't help that beyond the gate were some trees that would make easy hiding places for anyone trying to get onto the ranch.

"Is it the kidnappers?" Cassidy asked. She was already breathing through her mouth. Already terrified. And she had the baby clutched protectively in her arms while she rocked her.

Sawyer had to shake his head. "It might be nothing." And he prayed that was true.

He kept watch, but the only movement he saw was the wind rifling through the tree branches. Still, that didn't mean someone wasn't out there.

Sawyer had no idea how long it had been before Mason or someone in the house had noticed a triggered sensor. Maybe minutes. But even seconds were plenty long enough for someone to break the lock on the gate, get onto the ranch and take cover so they wouldn't be spotted.

Because he had his attention nailed to the area by the

fence, he got a serious shot of adrenaline when his phone vibrated again. Without taking his eyes off the fence, he answered the call.

"Bad news," Mason said. "Two men dressed all in black. They're hard as hell to see, but they're out there. I got several hands on the way now to help you."

"Thanks," Sawyer mumbled, and he glanced back at Cassidy. There were too many windows in the kitchen. Too many in the bedrooms, as well.

"Take Emma into the hall bathroom," Sawyer instructed her. "Get in the bathtub with her and stay put."

"But what about you?" she asked.

"I need to stay here. Don't worry. Both the front and back doors are locked. Windows, too. Plus, the security system is still turned on. If anyone tries to get in, the alarm will sound."

The assurance had barely left his mouth when he heard a sound he didn't want to hear. A soft thump. Not at the back of the house but at the side where there was a line of bedroom windows.

And the bathroom.

"Change of plan," Sawyer told Cassidy. "Get on the floor on the other side of the fridge." It wasn't ideal, but it was better than sending Cassidy anywhere near those windows.

She hurried to the fridge and sank onto the floor with her back against the wall. The baby started to fuss even more, and Cassidy continued to rock her while she mumbled something. A prayer, from the sound of it. Good. Because Sawyer wouldn't mind a little divine intervention. Anything to keep Cassidy and the baby safe.

The waiting began, and Sawyer tried to tamp down the adrenaline that was already sky high. His body was in fight mode, but it wasn't a fight he wanted. Not with these stakes.

Even over the baby's fussing, Sawyer heard another sound.

Breaking glass.

Followed by the frantic beeping of his security system. A warning that one of the windows had just been opened.

The intruders were in the house.

Sawyer didn't take the time to call Mason. Backup was already on the way, but it might not arrive soon enough. He had to take measures now to protect Cassidy and the baby.

"This way," he mouthed to her and tipped his head to the laundry room just off the kitchen. It had a door that led to the side yard, but he wasn't sure he could move her there just yet. Not until he figured out the position of the two men.

Sawyer kept Cassidy behind him, and he hurried to the keypad on the wall and pressed in the buttons to stop the alarm from sounding. It would only make the baby fuss more, and the noise would make it impossible for him to pinpoint the location of the men. He definitely wouldn't be able to hear footsteps and movement.

Even without the steady beeps of the security system pulsing through the house, Sawyer still didn't hear the intruders. They certainly hadn't come in with guns blazing, which told him this might be another kidnapping attempt.

But why would they want Cassidy when she'd already agreed to give them the ransom money?

"Ryland?" a man called out. Judging from the sound of his voice, he was either in one of the bedrooms or the hall.

Way too close.

Sawyer didn't answer because he didn't want to give

away their position. He only hoped that backup would arrive before this turned even uglier than it already was.

"Agent Ryland?" the man repeated. "We know you're there. We know you have the kid, too."

"It's one of the kidnappers who took Bennie and me," Cassidy whispered. "I recognize his voice."

Not much of a surprise that the kidnappers would come after them again, but it did make Sawyer wonder— where the heck was Bennie?

"Hand the kid over to us," the man shouted, "and you can keep Cassidy."

It was an interesting demand, one that Sawyer wouldn't even consider. No way would he turn over the baby to these goons. Still, it added another question to this dangerous situation.

Why did they want the child?

Unfortunately, Sawyer could think of a reason.

If Emma was indeed his daughter, they could use the baby to get money from him. He wasn't nearly as rich as Cassidy, but his grandparents had left him and his brother a good nest egg. Plus, his Ryland cousins were well off. Maybe the kidnappers figured they could milk Sawyer and his extended family in addition to the ransom that Cassidy would be paying for Bennie.

"You've got ten seconds to make up your mind," the kidnapper warned him.

Heaven knows what these men planned to do, and Sawyer didn't want to find out. He looked over Cassidy's shoulder and into the side yard. No sign of any backup. Going out there with Cassidy and the baby could be risky, but it might be safer than staying put.

Sawyer watched and listened for any movement of the

kidnappers. He finally heard footsteps, cautious and slow. They were making their way toward them.

He reached around Cassidy, unlocked the side door and then quickly changed positions with her so he could go outside first. Sawyer's gaze flew all around, and when he didn't see anyone, he pulled Cassidy into the yard with him.

They'd barely had time to take a step when a man came barreling out of the bedroom window. Sawyer took aim, fired, but he didn't hang around out in the open to see if he'd hit him. He pushed Cassidy and the baby around the corner and to the back of the house.

Just as the shot came his way.

Sawyer had hoped these bozos wouldn't fire around the baby, but obviously he'd hoped wrong. That shot was quickly followed by another one, and it took off a chunk of limestone siding.

"Get down on the ground," Sawyer told Cassidy.

She did, and unlike the gunmen, she wasn't putting the baby at risk. Cassidy sheltered Emma with her own body, and Sawyer did the same for both of them.

"Sawyer?" he heard Mason shout.

Backup, finally, and from the sound of his voice, Mason wasn't that far away. Somewhere near the front of the house. The kidnappers must have realized that, too, because he heard one of them curse.

"Here," Sawyer called out to Mason. And he leaned out to take another shot at the guy by the window.

Except he was no longer there.

It had only been a few seconds since Sawyer had last seen him, and since he was nowhere in the yard, that meant he'd gone back inside.

"Stay down," Sawyer whispered to Cassidy, and he

angled his body so he could keep watch on the side and back of the house. He braced himself for the two kidnappers to come rushing out the door.

But there were no sounds of footsteps. No more shots. However, there was something.

Smoke.

It started to seep beneath the back door, and the morning breeze blew it right toward them. This had to be some kind of trick to get them to move out into the open, and Sawyer had to make sure it didn't turn deadly.

His phone vibrated, but he didn't want to take his eyes off their surroundings to answer it. Instead, he tossed it down to Cassidy.

"Mason's covering the front of your house," she relayed to him a few seconds later.

Good. That meant these idiots wouldn't have an easy getaway. But Sawyer needed to capture them alive so he could force one of them to tell him what the devil was going on.

The seconds crawled by, and he could have sworn he heard each one tick off in his head. Every muscle in his body was stiff, primed for the fight, but nothing happened. Well, nothing other than the smoke that continued to billow right at them. It was just thick enough to make it hard to breathe.

Cassidy coughed and tried to cover the baby's face with her hand. It was only a temporary measure though. They couldn't stay much longer because the smoke could harm the baby. Unfortunately, moving came with its own set of risks since he didn't know which door or window the kidnappers would use to escape.

Sawyer glanced behind him at the SUV he'd driven from the main house. It wasn't an ideal location, but it would get Cassidy and the baby a little farther from the smoke, and he'd still be able to keep watch for the kidnappers. The men must have brought gas masks with them or they'd only set the fire by the back door.

Sawyer caught onto Cassidy's arm, helped her to her feet and got them moving in the direction of the SUV.

"Look out!" Mason shouted. Sawyer couldn't see his cousin, but he could hear him loud and clear. "They're on the roof."

Hell. Sawyer hadn't thought to look for them there, but he should have. There was access to the attic in the hall ceiling, and once there, the men would have been able to break through a wooden ventilation duct to get onto the roof.

And then escape.

Sawyer needed to stop that from happening.

He got Cassidy and the baby to the side of the SUV, maneuvering them onto the ground so he could crouch in front of them.

A shot cracked through the air.

Sawyer braced himself for it to come his way, but he realized it had been fired toward the front of the house. Maybe by Mason. Or *at* him. Sawyer wanted to help his cousin, but he couldn't leave Cassidy. Especially since the baby was the kidnapper's primary target.

Another shot.

Sawyer still couldn't see Mason or the two men, but he heard the footsteps. Someone was running, not toward him. But away from the house.

The sun was up just enough for him to see the shadowy figure running toward the ranch trail. That was no doubt where the men had left their vehicle. But before Sawyer could get off a shot, the man ducked behind the side of the barn.

There was movement on the other side of the house.

More footsteps. And the sound of someone cursing. It wasn't Mason's voice, and that meant it was the kidnapper's.

The man bolted out from the side of Sawyer's house and tried to make a beeline for the fence. However, this time, Sawyer did have the shot.

He didn't go for the kill. He wanted this guy alive, so he fired a shot into his leg. The man cursed again, growling in pain, but he dropped to the ground.

"I've got him covered," Mason said, hurrying toward the downed man. He pointed his gun at him and kicked the man's own weapon from his hand. His cousin then took out his phone and called the fire department.

Maybe they'd get there in time to save his house.

Sawyer's attention shifted to the barn, toward the other man, but he was already too late. In the distance he heard the sound of someone starting a car engine. The kidnapper, no doubt. By the time Sawyer could get to him, he'd be long gone.

But not his partner.

"Stay close to me," Sawyer told Cassidy.

He didn't want to leave her by the SUV in case the other kidnapper backtracked, and he didn't want her too close to the burning house. However, he did need to get a better look at the kidnapper to see if he recognized him.

The guy was heavily muscled and bald. He looked like a thug. But not a thug that Sawyer knew. The guy was a stranger.

"Start talking," Sawyer said. He, too, pointed his gun at the man on the ground. The guy was bleeding. Cursing, too.

However, he didn't appear to be on the verge of confessing anything. That wasn't a look of surrender he gave

Sawyer. Just the opposite. He grimaced and smiled at the same time.

But his attention didn't go to Sawyer.

It went to Cassidy.

"You have no idea what you've just done," the man growled. "You just signed your brother's death warrant."

Chapter Eight

The kidnapper's words kept going nonstop through Cassidy's head.

You just signed your brother's death warrant.

She prayed that wasn't true, but so far neither Sawyer nor she had been able to figure out if it had been an empty threat. That's because the kidnapper had lawyered up as soon as they had all arrived at the sheriff's office, and while he was waiting for his attorney to show up, the man had refused to give them his name or say anything else.

Unlike Sawyer.

He'd had plenty to say, but most of it had been to berate himself for not taking more security precautions to keep the baby and her safe. Cassidy wasn't sure more precautions would have helped since the men seemed hell-bent on kidnapping her again.

Or maybe they'd only planned to kidnap Emma.

If that was true, then it wasn't safe for the baby to be placed in foster care. And that's why Sawyer had been on the phone most of the morning, arranging for a safe house and a nanny-bodyguard for the little girl.

For now, though, they were in wait mode.

Waiting for the safe house to be ready. Waiting for the kidnapper to talk. And waiting on a call about Bennie's ransom.

Cassidy figured the last item was a long shot since they had one of the kidnappers in custody, but it was possible the second kidnapper would still make a ransom demand while adding a condition that his partner be released, as well. She seriously doubted that Sawyer would give in to a demand like that.

And it put her brother in even more danger.

That cut her to the core, and she tried to steady her nerves to stop herself from panicking. The baby helped. With Sawyer and his cousins busy with the investigation and safe-house arrangements, Cassidy had been the one to feed and change Emma. And even though the child had fallen asleep again, Cassidy continued to hold her while she paced and worried. Just having Emma in her arms stopped her from falling apart.

Sawyer finished his latest call, and he blew out a weary breath before his gaze came to hers. "The bodyguard will be here soon to take Emma and you to the safe house."

Cassidy was so exhausted that it took her a moment to realize what was missing from his comment. "And what about you? You're not coming with us?"

Sawyer paused, got up from his brother's desk, where he'd been sitting, and walked to her. "I need to stay here and try to coax our friend into confessing."

He hiked his thumb toward the interview room across the hall where the bald kidnapper was waiting for the D.A. to charge him with assorted felonies. Once his lawyer showed up, they could continue to press the man for info about her brother's whereabouts and any other details about the case. And it wasn't unreasonable that Sawyer would be the one who'd do the pressing. After all, he was a federal agent, and this was part of his job. Still, it didn't feel reasonable to her right now since it would mean going to the safe house without him.

Sawyer gave another of those weary breaths, and ran his hand down her arm. It was soothing but not nearly enough.

"What if the kidnappers come after Emma and me again?" She didn't wait for him to answer. "If that happens, I'd rather you be there."

"Yeah." And that's all he said for several moments, though their gazes continued to hold. He leaned in, gave her another arm rub. "I'll finish up here and may be able to get out to the safe house before nightfall."

Even though he probably hadn't meant that to sound intimate, it did. Of course, everything he said and did fell into that category. This heat between them wasn't cooling down much.

"Yeah," he repeated, and she figured from the sizzle in his eyes, they were having the same bad thoughts.

He tore his gaze from hers and looked down at the baby. "You won't have to tend to her—"

"I want to," Cassidy interrupted, obviously surprising Sawyer. Surprising herself, too.

"Just don't get too attached," he added. "If she's not mine, we'll need to find her parents."

"Too late. I'm already attached."

He mumbled another "yeah" and brushed a kiss on the baby's cheek.

Then Cassidy's.

Sawyer pulled back as if to hurry away to make another call, but he didn't. He leaned in and this time brushed a kiss on her mouth. There it was again. The trickle of heat that went from her lips to her toes. It was potent stuff, and it made her head even fuzzier than it already was.

"This can't go anywhere," he mumbled seconds after delivering that mind-blowing kiss.

"I know." And she did know, but Cassidy was having a hard time remembering that Sawyer was never going to believe that she hadn't slept with him only to get information. Repeating the mistake would only make matters worse.

There was a rap at the door a split second before it opened, and Grayson stuck his head inside. He opened his mouth but didn't say anything at first. Instead, his attention landed on the close contact between them.

Sawyer quickly stepped away.

"We took the kidnapper's prints and got a match," Grayson said. "His name is Chester Finley." He looked at her as if he expected her to recognize the name.

She didn't. "Who is he?"

"A career criminal, for one thing. But he also worked for you a few weeks back. He was part of a landscaping crew."

Cassidy still had to shake her head. "I was away on business looking at some ranch properties when the crew did the work." But it sickened her to think this monster had been so close to Bennie and her. "You think Finley was there so he could spy on us?"

Sawyer made a sound of agreement. "Who hired the crew?"

"Kevin Amerson. He's been my household manager for years, and I trust him completely. Kevin wouldn't have knowingly hired a criminal. Especially one like Chester Finley."

Still, Grayson jotted down Kevin's name and would no doubt question him. It likely wouldn't lead anywhere, but maybe Kevin would remember something about the man. Something they could use to find out the name of his partner. Also, Grayson would need to rule out for certain that Kevin wasn't involved in the kidnappings.

When Grayson finished with his notes, he looked up as if to ask her another question, but the bell jangled over the front door, and he turned his attention in that direction. His eyes widened, and he shoved the notepad into his pocket and hurried toward the reception area.

Grayson also drew his gun.

That put her heart right in her throat, especially when Sawyer pulled his, as well, and practically jumped in front of her. Cassidy braced herself for the sounds of shots and prepared for another attack. Had the second kidnapper come to try to rescue his partner? If so, this could turn deadly fast.

But there were no shots.

"Call an ambulance," Grayson shouted.

"Stay here," Sawyer told her, and he, too, headed for the reception area.

When Sawyer and she had come through there earlier, Bree had been manning the desk. She hoped the deputy was still there in case Sawyer and Grayson needed backup.

Cassidy pulled the baby close to her, held her breath and waited. Still no sounds of an attack, but she heard a voice. Someone moaning as if in pain.

"My sister," someone said. "Where is she?"

Even though the man had spoken in a broken whisper, Cassidy had no trouble recognizing the voice.

Bennie.

She bolted from the room, and the moment she was in the hall, Cassidy saw him. His face was bloody and bruised, and his gaze connected with hers.

Before her brother collapsed.

SAWYER MANAGED TO CATCH Bennie before his head hit the tile floor.

Bennie's breathing was shallow, and his face looked as if he'd been on the receiving end of a good beating, but Sawyer couldn't see any obvious life-threatening injuries. That didn't mean there weren't any, because Bennie was also clutching his chest.

"Cassidy," Bennie said, his voice weak and practically soundless.

Still, Cassidy managed to hear him just fine, because she bolted from the office and hurried toward her brother. As soon as she handed Bree the baby, she knelt on the floor and touched her fingers to her brother's bloodied face.

"What happened to you? Who did this?" Unlike Bennie, Cassidy's voice had plenty of sound, and Sawyer could hear the tears threatening. It didn't take long before one of those tears spilled down her cheek.

"The kidnapper..." And that's all Bennie said for several snail-crawling moments. "He was furious when Sawyer arrested his partner, and he beat me. Tried to kill me, too."

So, Finley's threat about signing her brother's death warrant had partially come true. But obviously, the kidnapper hadn't succeeded.

"Who's the kidnapper?" Sawyer demanded.

Bennie shook his head. "I don't know. I never got a look at his face. I'm glad they didn't take you and the baby," Bennie continued, looking straight at Cassidy.

"But why did they want us?" Cassidy asked. "I told them I'd pay the ransom."

Bennie gave a weak nod. "They said the baby was their insurance to make sure you paid."

Well, it would have been good insurance, all right. Cassidy hardly knew the baby, but she hadn't lied about the attachment to Emma. She would no doubt pay anything to keep the child and her brother safe. Still, a kidnapping attempt seemed a big risk just to get some insurance.

"How'd you get away from him?" Sawyer asked.

Cassidy shot him a back-off glance and slid her hand behind her brother's head to cradle it. But Sawyer had no intention of backing off. A woman was dead, and Bennie had been kidnapped. Plus, there was the baby. Sawyer needed answers, and the most likely person to have those answers was Bennie.

"When the kidnapper got a call," Bennie said, "he was distracted, so I got up and ran." He shook his head, pulled in some labored breaths. "I didn't have a phone and was afraid to go on the roads for fear he'd find me. So I just kept walking until I got to town."

Later, Sawyer would want more details about that escape and where Bennie had been held, but he had to do this pseudointerrogation fast since he could already hear sirens in the distance. The ambulance was on its way. Once Bennie was at the hospital, it might be hours before Sawyer could question him again, especially if the man had serious injuries.

"What about April Warrick?" Sawyer pressed. "Why did the kidnapper take her, and is this baby hers?"

"I don't know." A moment later, Bennie repeated it. "The kidnappers were already holding April and the baby hostage by the time they grabbed me." Bennie turned his head and stared at Sawyer. "I heard them say that April's baby is yours, and they were going to use the kid to extort money from you."

Well, that explained the kidnapping attempt. Maybe

the men hadn't come to take Cassidy at all. Emma could have been the sole target. That didn't help with the knot in Sawyer's gut.

"I never slept with April," Sawyer insisted.

But Bennie only shook his head. "The kidnappers were certain you had."

Well, they were dead wrong. Still, he wasn't sure people would believe it. Those DNA test results couldn't come back fast enough. Of course, they might just prove the baby was his, but even so, that would mean the test would prove April wasn't the mother.

Monica Barnes would be.

And if she was, then Sawyer had to wonder what had happened to her.

Had the kidnappers murdered Monica, too?

It turned his stomach to think that could have happened because of her involvement with him, but at least they had one of the kidnappers in custody. Too bad Sawyer couldn't beat the truth out of him.

"Who killed April?" Sawyer asked, though he figured the answer was obvious.

The kidnappers had.

Still, Bennie didn't get a chance to respond because the wail of sirens got louder, and the ambulance braked to a stop directly in front of the door. The medics got out and brought a gurney in with them.

"You'll be fine," Cassidy said to her brother. "You'll get the medical treatment you need, and then we can talk when you're feeling up to it."

A medic moved between Cassidy and Bennie, but Bennie craned his neck so he could see his sister. "Talk? About what?"

Her gaze drifted back to the interrogation room. "About the kidnapping. And the man they have in custody. Chester Finley. He worked for us for a while." She shook her head. "But all of that can wait."

Yeah, it could, but not for long. Cassidy didn't come out and say it, but it sounded as if she might have some doubts about her brother. And with good reason. Maybe Bennie knew Finley and had done something that had prompted Finley to kidnap him.

But what?

With Bennie's history of illegal deals, Sawyer figured money had to play into the motive.

The medics took Bennie's blood pressure and examined his eyes. "Are you hurting anywhere?" one of them asked Bennie.

"Just my face and chest. They hit me pretty hard."

They had, but maybe his injuries weren't life threatening. The medics lifted Bennie onto the gurney and were about to take him outside to the ambulance, when the door flew open and trouble walked in.

Willy Malloy.

"I was at the diner across the street," Willy snapped, and his narrowed eyes went to Bennie. "I thought it was that low-life scum, Bennie O'Neal, and I was right."

Cassidy shook her head and looked at Sawyer, no doubt for answers as to why Willy had that dangerous look in his eyes. A look aimed at Bennie.

"What do you want?" Sawyer demanded from Willy.

But Willy didn't answer. He reached past the medic and caught onto the front of Bennie's shirt. "I'm not letting you leave until you tell me the truth about April's death," Willy growled.

Bennie's eyes widened. "I don't know what you mean."

"Yeah, you do," Willy insisted. "I know it was you who killed her, and I sure as hell can prove it."

Chapter Nine

Cassidy took hold of Willy and pulled him off her brother. Not that she had to do it alone. Sawyer shoved Willy to the side, and the man would have fallen if he hadn't caught onto the window to steady himself.

Willy aimed some of his venom at Sawyer that seconds earlier he'd doled out to Bennie. But it wasn't the venom that bothered her.

It was the accusation of murder that Willy had made against her brother.

"You're lying," Bennie snarled, and despite his injuries, he managed to sound surprisingly strong when he spoke to Willy. "Because I didn't kill April."

"You did, too. I know it was you." Willy tried to go at Bennie again, but Sawyer not only held him back, he slammed him hard against the wall. Thankfully, Bree took the baby out of the area and into Grayson's office. There was no need for Emma to hear all of this yelling.

"Use your inside voice," Sawyer warned Willy in a mocking tone. "And keep your temper in check."

Cassidy appreciated that Sawyer seemed to be taking her brother's side in this, but that probably didn't mean he thought Bennie was innocent. He despised her brother, but at the moment he despised Willy even more.

Willy didn't try to move closer to her brother again,

but he did stab his index finger in Bennie's direction. "He's the one you should be yelling at so you can get him to confess. He killed April, all right."

"You said there was proof?" Sawyer reminded Willy, and he motioned for the medics to stay put.

"Yeah. April told me she was scared of this clown, that he'd threatened her to keep her mouth shut when he broke off things with her. Guess he didn't want his new girlfriend to get word of it. I wasn't the only one who heard it. That quack shrink heard it, too. Two witnesses saying the same thing, and that's proof, if you ask me."

"Really?" Cassidy asked, and she didn't bother to keep the skepticism out of her voice. "Because we heard that the person April was afraid of was *you*."

Willy didn't jump to deny it, but he shot her a glare. "You're just trying to protect your brother." The glare then went to Sawyer. "Got your FBI friend here still helping you, too, I see. But I got news for both of you— Bennie killed her, all right, and he'll do the same to anybody who gets in his way."

"I didn't kill her," Bennie repeated.

He groaned, closed his eyes a moment as if reliving some horrible memories. Cassidy had some of those same memories of being held captive, of thinking that Bennie and she might be killed at any moment. At least she hoped that's all there was to his reaction.

"Are you in pain?" she asked him.

Bennie took his time answering. "Some. But I won't let that get in the way of learning the truth. And something tells me that Willy knows a lot when it comes to the truth."

Willy immediately challenged that. Not with a shout. Probably because Sawyer was still practically in his face. But the man mumbled plenty of profanity.

Sawyer ignored him and turned his attention back to Bennie. "What did happen to April?"

"I'm not sure. After Cassidy left to get the photo of the baby with you, one of the kidnappers stepped out of the building for a few minutes, and he came back in with April."

Cassidy met her brother's gaze. "Had April recently given birth?"

"I don't know. And since she was wearing a loose top, it was hard to tell."

So, she'd already delivered because it would have been easy to see a nine-month baby bump. Did that mean Emma was indeed April's baby? It seemed likely that the kidnappers would have taken April's newborn when they'd kidnapped her.

"April didn't mention the baby?" Sawyer wanted to know.

Bennie shook his head. "But she was furious that the men had taken her. Several times she said that Willy was behind this."

"Not me!" Willy howled. "He's lying—"

Sawyer cut off anything else with a glare. It worked. Willy shut up and backed away, though he did continue to mumble more profanity and profess his innocence.

"April thought Willy had kidnapped us so he could get revenge for her cheating on him with me," Bennie went on. "She was afraid that once Willy got his hands on the ransom money, he'd kill us all. So we waited until the kidnappers were distracted with a phone call, and April cut me loose from the ropes, and we tried to escape."

That must have happened just minutes before Sawyer and she had arrived back at the Tumbleweed.

"April cut you loose?" Sawyer questioned. "How? With what?"

Part of her wanted to stop these questions and get Bennie to the hospital, but her brother no longer seemed in pain. In fact, he sat up even farther to answer Sawyer. "She had a knife hidden under her top. I didn't ask her where she got it. I was just thankful to be out of those ropes."

"What happened next?" Sawyer asked when Bennie didn't say anything else.

"I'm not sure. It was raining, and when we were running, April and I got separated in the woods. I figured that she'd managed to get away, but one of the kidnappers found me. I think it's the one you have in custody now. He put a gun to my head and dragged me back to where they'd left their vehicles. It wasn't long before I heard a shot."

Yes, Cassidy had heard it, too, and she'd thought her brother had been killed.

Bennie swallowed hard. "When the other kidnapper came back, April wasn't with him, and he had blood on his clothes."

It was so hard for Cassidy to hear all of this. From the moment Bennie and she had been taken captive, she'd been terrified that someone would die.

And it had happened.

Still, there was something about all of this that didn't make sense. "Why did the kidnappers have me take the baby to Sawyer for that photograph?" she asked.

"I figured it was because Sawyer was the baby's father, and they wanted to milk some money out of him, too. Maybe they planned to use the photo to show his boss or something. It wouldn't have looked good for an FBI agent to have fathered a baby with a woman with a criminal record who was now dead. Murdered, at that."

No, it wouldn't have looked good. But that meant the

kidnappers must have truly believed that Sawyer was Emma's father. Or else they simply wanted to make it look that way.

Oh, mercy.

Maybe the photo was meant to give Sawyer a motive for killing April.

One glance at Sawyer, and she realized he'd already come to the same conclusion. Even if he wasn't Emma's father, it might look as if he'd murdered April when she tried to blackmail him with the child.

But Sawyer wouldn't have done that.

Cassidy wanted to feel the same way about her brother. And she did, for the most part anyway. However, she still had that niggling feeling that there was something Bennie wasn't telling her. Probably because Bennie had a history of keeping things from her and involving himself with the wrong people.

Bennie's attention shifted back to Willy. "Or maybe the kidnappings, the photo, all of this was just a way for you to get more revenge on another of April's lovers."

"April and I weren't lovers," Sawyer snapped.

"But he thought you were." Bennie tipped his head to Willy. "And when it comes to April, Willy would do just about anything to get back at her. Including murder."

"If I'd wanted revenge," Willy quickly answered, "you damn sure wouldn't be here talking about it. You'd already be in the grave."

"Enough of this," Sawyer growled, and he motioned for the medics to get moving. Cassidy tried to follow, but Sawyer stopped her. "The kidnapper could come after you at the hospital."

Cassidy shook her head. "But what about Bennie? The kidnapper could come after him, too."

"I'll arrange for some security," Grayson said, taking

out his phone. He made the call as Cassidy watched the ambulance drive away.

The moment that Grayson was finished with his call, he took Willy by the arm. "Come on. I want you to stay put until I have someone at the hospital. Wouldn't want you to carry your fight with Bennie there, especially after that *in the grave* comment you just made."

Good. The last thing her brother needed was another confrontation with this hothead. Too bad Grayson and Sawyer didn't have any evidence to arrest Willy.

Or maybe they did.

"Can you use any of what my brother said to charge Willy with kidnapping?" she asked. Yes, it was a long shot, but she wanted Willy locked up.

Grayson blew out a long breath, shook his head. "But with his temper, maybe he'll do something stupid that will give me cause to arrest him."

That sounded like a veiled threat. It must have sounded like one to Willy, too, because he shut up and let Grayson lead him to one of the interrogation rooms. He deposited Willy inside, shut the door and came back to reception. Still holding the baby, Bree came out, as well.

Sawyer checked the time. "I need to get Cassidy and the baby to the safe house. Once the bodyguards and nanny are in place, I'll come back here and try to get Finley to talk."

"No need," Grayson said, glancing at Cassidy. He no doubt saw the worry and fatigue in her eyes. "Stay with them for the night. Maybe by tomorrow we'll find the other kidnapper, and the danger will be over."

Cassidy latched on to that hope, but Sawyer certainly wasn't following suit. He volleyed glances between her and the interview room, and he finally scrubbed his hand over his face.

"I'll be back first thing in the morning," he told Grayson.

Which meant they'd be spending another night under the same roof. Of course, they wouldn't be alone this time, not to mention the baby would be with them. Maybe that would be enough to cool down the fire brewing between them.

"You can drive to the safe house in my SUV," Bree volunteered. "It already has an infant seat in it."

Sawyer thanked her and took her keys when Bree pulled them from her pocket. She also eased the baby into Cassidy's waiting arms.

"You'll call as soon as you find out about Bennie's injuries?" Cassidy asked.

Grayson nodded. However, he didn't get to add more because his phone rang. Sawyer started to lead her toward the back exit, but Grayson held up his finger in a wait-a-moment gesture. He grabbed a notepad and started writing.

Cassidy couldn't hear any part of the conversation or see what he was jotting down, but whatever the caller was saying, it had captured Grayson's complete attention. She prayed it wasn't more bad news because they'd already had enough of that for the day.

"She's what?" Grayson asked. "How the hell did that happen?"

Sawyer groaned. Yes, this was definitely bad news, and all Sawyer and she could do was wait for Grayson to deliver it.

"Thank you for getting Willy off my brother," Cassidy whispered to Sawyer while Grayson continued his conversation. "I know that couldn't have been easy for you."

He didn't deny it. And Sawyer paused a long time. "Willy could be right about Bennie. Or vice versa," he quickly added.

Cassidy nodded, prayed he was wrong about Bennie. "At least part of the danger is over. We have one kidnapper in custody, and with Bennie free, there's no way they can collect the ransom money."

"The danger's still there," Sawyer argued. "I hope I'm wrong, but I doubt whoever's behind this will just give up on getting the other half million." He looked down at the baby. "To get their hands on the cash, they'll no doubt try to kidnap Bennie, you or Emma."

"Or you," she added.

He flinched a little, shook his head.

"You," she verified. "Willy thinks we're lovers. I could see that in his eyes. And if he believes it, so could the kidnapper."

"You'd pay a half million for me?" Sawyer asked with a Texas-size amount of skepticism in his voice.

"Yes." And she didn't have to think about it. "This doesn't have to do with that night we spent together." At least she hoped it didn't. "But you saved my life and Emma's today."

Sawyer stared at her. Cursed. "That is *not* going to happen between us again."

She nodded. "I know."

But Cassidy figured just saying it wouldn't stop her from wanting it to happen.

"The cops just finished going through April's apartment," Grayson said the moment he ended the call.

Good. With everything else going on, Cassidy had forgotten all about the search warrant. Now she braced herself for whatever had put that scowl on Grayson's face.

"They found April's diary taped behind her headboard," Grayson explained. "It's over a hundred pages, so it'll take them a while to go through it all, but my brother Nate spotted something right away."

Cassidy prayed that Grayson wasn't about to say it was an incriminating entry regarding her brother.

"It's about Dr. Diane Blackwell," Grayson continued.

Not her brother. But that didn't mean there wasn't something else about Bennie in there.

"If the diary is really April's, then Willy didn't lie about April being afraid of the shrink." Grayson looked down at his notes. "The last entry that April made said 'I think Dr. Blackwell is playing with my mind somehow. Maybe even slipping me drugs during our sessions. I think she might be trying to kill me or something,'" he finished.

Cassidy replayed all of that in her mind and then shook her head. "Maybe April was just being paranoid. Because what motive would Dr. Blackwell have for doing that?"

Now it was Grayson's turn to shake his head. "I don't know, but it's definitely something we need to check out. We also need to make sure the diary is real and wasn't planted by one of the kidnappers."

True, she wouldn't put it past Willy to do something like that.

Sawyer took out his phone. "I'll get Dr. Blackwell out here."

"You can't," Grayson said. "Well, not right away. Nate made some calls, and according to her coworkers, Dr. Blackwell's missing."

Chapter Ten

Sawyer went through his security checklist one more time.

There was a fellow agent in the living room watching the front of the house. Another one was in his car parked at the back of the house. The nanny, Elaine Wilkins, was from a P.I. agency that specialized in providing bodyguard services to infants at risk. She would spend the night in Emma's room in case something went wrong.

He hoped like the devil that it didn't.

Both Emma and Cassidy had already been through enough.

He checked the security system again to make sure it was armed. It was. All the blinds were down, and once it got dark, they'd use minimal lighting so they wouldn't draw attention to themselves. Not that there would be a lot of opportunities for them to draw attention. The house was out in the middle of nowhere, centered on about fifty acres. It had once been a ranch, but now it would hopefully be a safe haven until the second kidnapper was caught. Then Cassidy and Emma could go home.

Wherever home was in Emma's case.

Sawyer had already called about the DNA results, only to be told they weren't ready. Nothing unusual about that, but he had asked that the test be expedited. If he wasn't Emma's father, then he needed to look for her parents.

Just the thought of that twisted his stomach, but it had to be done. If she were his, he certainly wouldn't want anyone keeping her from him.

He heard the footsteps and saw Cassidy making her way into the kitchen and toward him. "Emma's okay," she relayed.

Like Sawyer, Cassidy had obviously been going through her own mental list, and that included frequent checks to the makeshift nursery to ensure that Emma was still safe. Sawyer had made a few of those trips himself, and with each one he'd studied that tiny, precious face to see if he could pick out any resemblance to himself.

He couldn't.

But that didn't mean she wasn't his. Hell, he could hardly remember Monica's face, and it was entirely possible that Emma looked exactly like her mom.

"It'll be okay," Cassidy said.

She had a death grip on a glass of iced tea she'd been nursing, and her reassurance didn't mesh with the fear he saw in her eyes. The same fear had been there when he'd tried to reassure her on the drive to the safe house. Nothing would truly be okay until this ordeal was over.

"Anything in your phone calls about Monica Barnes?" she asked.

Sawyer had to shake his head. "No one knows where she is." Like Dr. Blackwell, Monica was missing.

Well, maybe.

And maybe Monica just didn't want to be found. There could be plenty of reasons for that, but he hoped it wasn't because she didn't want anything to do with a baby they'd possibly made together. Too bad he didn't know Monica well enough to believe she wouldn't do something like that.

"If I ever get the urge to have another one-night stand," he mumbled, "I hope someone hits me in the head with a rock."

The corner of Cassidy's mouth twitched a little as if threatening to smile, but she clamped her teeth over her bottom lip until the moment passed. Considering he'd had a one-nighter with her, Cassidy probably thought he was reckless. And sometimes he was.

He'd been especially reckless with her.

He darn sure should have learned about her lawbreaking sibling before he'd ever stripped off her clothes and gotten her into bed.

"Maybe you can ask for references from your next lover," she mumbled. Obviously she hadn't fully fought back that urge to poke some fun at him. "Or do an FBI background check."

"Kinda takes the spontaneity out of it." Something he wished he hadn't said. It was just another reminder of his night with Cassidy. And the kiss. And the dozen or more heated looks they'd given each other since all this kidnapping mess had started.

Like now, for instance.

That was definitely a heated look. One he felt in every stupid part of his body.

As if she knew exactly what he was thinking, Cassidy cleared her throat. "What about Bennie?" she asked. "Anything more on his condition?"

Another head shake. "Only that his injuries aren't serious." The doctor was keeping him at the hospital for a while only because he was dehydrated.

In the grand scheme of things, Bennie had gotten off lightly with just a few stitches and some bruises. Cassidy and he had gotten off lightly, too, but for Cassidy, the attack would no doubt be the stuff of nightmares for a long time. Heck, it would give Sawyer a few nightmares, too. He'd come close to losing both Emma and Cassidy, and he couldn't be sure that another close call wasn't out there waiting for them.

Since the thoughts and worries were gnawing away at him—the blasted heat between them, too—Sawyer focused on what he could do something about.

"You should try to eat," Sawyer reminded her. The fridge was fully stocked with plenty of sandwiches and frozen food, and since he'd been with Cassidy all day, he knew she hadn't eaten a bite.

"Maybe later," she mumbled.

Even though he figured she'd said that just to placate him, he didn't push it. Truth was, he'd had to force himself to eat earlier. His stomach was still churning from the attack and the worry of a new one. Still, starving himself wasn't going to help anything.

Even though he figured it was a bad idea, Sawyer walked closer to her. For just a moment Cassidy stiffened a little. But this wasn't fear. Nope. She knew getting close was a bad idea, too.

Did that stop them?

Not a chance.

"Maybe you should start looking for that rock now," she whispered.

Sawyer couldn't help himself. He laughed. Why, he didn't know, because this wasn't a laughing situation. He slipped his arm around her waist and eased her to him. He hoped it would help soothe both their raw nerves, but he purposely didn't put his mouth anywhere near hers.

"Funny, I keep finding myself in this position," she said, leaning back just a little so they were face-to-face.

Obviously, she wasn't thinking of the danger of their mouths being too close. "In your arms, with you comforting me. And there's never a rock in sight."

Yes, it had happened a couple of times. And sadly, it hadn't always been for comfort. Like that whole session earlier and the one the year before when they'd landed in bed.

That jolted him back to reality, and Sawyer moved farther from her.

Her eyebrow lifted. The corner of her mouth, too. But there was no humor in her near smile, either. No doubt because she was remembering the yelling match that had followed the scalding-hot sex.

"I didn't, you know," she said almost in a whisper.

"Didn't what?"

But he wasn't sure he wanted to hear the answer. In fact, Sawyer wasn't sure he wanted to hear anything because it was likely to up the heat in his body. Anything would do it at this point.

Including Cassidy just breathing.

"I didn't sleep with you so I could find out about your investigation into Bennie's business dealings," she said.

There it was. The blasted gauntlet. They'd been dancing around it for days now, but he hadn't wanted it thrown because he didn't want to have to rehash that old argument.

That thought got him moving back even more, and Sawyer groaned. "I thought we agreed never to discuss that."

"No. You demanded we not discuss it, but I didn't agree. You need to hear this because it's the truth. I did arrange to meet you, but that was it."

She snagged his wrist to stop him from turning around. Sawyer could have broken the grip, easily, but he stayed there. Still standing too close. And having a conversation that would break down even more barriers than a kissing session.

"I didn't plan on doing anything other than talk to you," she continued. "But then the talking led to a few drinks…" Her words trailed off, thank goodness. No need to remind him where those few drinks had landed them.

"During all the *talking,* you might have mentioned that you were Bennie's sister," he reminded her.

She nodded. "And I intended to do that—"

"When? Before or after you let me get you naked?" Yeah, that was harsh, but that whole encounter was still a sore subject for him.

"Definitely before," she snapped. But almost immediately the angry expression faded, and she dodged his glare. "Look, I don't make a habit of sleeping with men I hardly know. Whether you believe it or not, you were my first and only one-night stand."

He did believe her. Didn't want to. But he did. Still, that didn't let her off the hook.

"You can't deny that you'd do anything to protect your brother," he reminded her.

"No. I can't deny that. And you no doubt feel the same way about your own brother."

He did. To an extent. He wouldn't break the law for him. Except Sawyer immediately had to rethink that. Blood was indeed thicker than the badge, and if it came down to saving his kid brother, he would do whatever it took. Hopefully, it wouldn't take sleeping with a woman. Even one who seemed to light every unwanted fire in his body.

"Yes," Cassidy said softly. "I didn't need a reason to sleep with you. The desire was already there. Still is."

Man, he would have liked to argue that, but she was

right about the blasted lingering attraction. It burned hot and showed no signs of letting up. So hot that Sawyer thought about kissing her again. And not just kissing. More.

Much more.

Thankfully, the sound of the ringing phone stopped the conversation and also stopped him from acting on the *much more*. But Sawyer was worried he would need more than a phone call to keep Cassidy out of his arms.

And his bed.

He glanced at the phone and answered it right away when he saw Grayson's name on the screen. "All settled in?" his cousin asked.

"Getting there. Everything okay?"

Sawyer didn't realize that he was holding his breath until his lungs started to ache. Cassidy seemed to be doing the same, and she leaned in, no doubt so she could hear. He made that easier for her by putting the call on Speaker.

"So far everything's okay," Grayson went on. "I just got a call from the doctor about Bennie. Within an hour or so, he'll be released into my protective custody."

Well, it wasn't bad news, but it could be. "You're not thinking of bringing him here?" No need to spell out that Sawyer didn't trust Cassidy's brother, and he'd yet to rule out Bennie's possible involvement in this. After all, Bennie had been involved with shady deals in the past. Yeah, his *involvement* would be extreme since he'd been beaten up and Cassidy had been kidnapped, too, but Sawyer wasn't about to eliminate Bennie as a suspect just yet.

Sawyer's gaze met Cassidy's, and he expected her to be riled about his request, but the fear and concern were still there.

No anger.

Of course, that particular emotion might come later — especially if there was another attempt to kidnap her brother.

"No, Bennie refused our offer of a safe house," Grayson verified. "He wants to go back to his place. He said he has a good security system, and I can assign someone to watch him."

"He'll probably try to ditch a guard," Cassidy volunteered. "I know my brother, and he'll want to go after the kidnapper. Please don't let that happen."

"We'll do our best," Grayson assured her. "I've also asked the FBI to flag bank deposits of half a million dollars. The ransom amount you've already paid. It's possible the kidnapper will try to deposit that money somewhere, and if he does, we can use that to track him down."

It was a good plan, but there were plenty of ways to hide money. Maybe the kidnapper wasn't smart enough to figure them out.

"What about Chester Finley?" Sawyer asked. "Is he talking yet?"

"Not a word. He'll be arraigned in a few hours. Maybe he'll ask for a plea deal once he realizes he's being charged with enough felonies to keep him in jail for the rest of his sorry life."

Maybe. Finley would perhaps rat out his partner so they could get to the bottom of this.

"We're still looking for Dr. Blackwell," Grayson continued. "Officially, she's not a missing person because it hasn't been twenty-four hours, but her coworkers said it wasn't like her not to show for work."

"What about her husband?" Sawyer asked. He remembered the whopping diamond ring she'd been wearing.

"That's sticky territory. His name is Martin Black-well. Ring any bells?"

Yeah, it did. "He's a rich businessman. Owns some hotels on the Riverwalk."

"That's the one," Grayson verified. "Diane and he are separated, and he's filed for divorce. A divorce she's fighting. From what I'm hearing, she ran through a boat-load of his money, and he's trying to ditch her before she goes through the rest. There's a prenup, so she won't be getting anything in the divorce."

The doc had a messy personal life. And combined with the allegations Willy had made against her, it set off the little alarm in his head. The timing of her disappearance was certainly suspicious, and he had to wonder if it had anything to do with the kidnapping.

"How long has she been missing exactly?" Sawyer asked.

"No one has seen her since her trip to Silver Creek."

Bad timing again. "Is her soon-to-be ex a suspect?"

"No. He's out of the country on business and is already in another relationship. A happy one, from the sound of it. If he had any part in her disappearance, I'd be surprised."

Sawyer would trust his cousin's judgment about that, but he went back to the timing again. The doc had dis-appeared shortly after her trip to the Silver Creek sher-iff's office. And Willy had been there. Sawyer hoped the doctor hadn't been kidnapped, too, by Willy or anyone else involved.

But then, why would the kidnappers have gone after her?

Unfortunately, Sawyer could think of a solid reason. "What about April's diary? Any other mention of Dr. Blackwell, maybe something about April being worried that the doc was going to do something bad to her—like kidnap her for ransom?"

Because if so, then maybe the doctor had disappeared rather than face an interrogation and possible criminal charges.

"There was nothing about the kidnapping in the diary," Grayson explained. "But Nate found an entry that was a little surprising. April thought Bennie and Dr. Blackwell were seeing each other. And I don't mean in a professional way. April thought they were lovers."

Well, that didn't paint a pretty picture of the doc, and he looked at Cassidy to see if she knew anything about a supposed relationship between Diane and her brother.

Cassidy just shook her head. "Bennie never mentioned her."

"But they had met," Sawyer reminded her. "Dr. Blackwell mentioned it when she was at the sheriff's office. She said she'd met you and your brother at a fund-raiser."

"Yes," Cassidy mumbled. And he could almost see the wheels turning in her head, trying to remember the details of that meeting. "If Bennie was seeing her, he didn't tell me. I'll call him and ask—"

"Already spoke to him about it," Grayson interrupted. "He said he knew her but they were never lovers. Apparently, April had a jealous streak and often accused Bennie of having affairs with other women—including Diane."

Sawyer thought about that a moment. "Maybe April was behind Bennie's kidnapping because she was jealous of the affair she believed he was having with her shrink? She could have hired Finley to help her, faked her own kidnapping, and then he could have double-crossed her. With her out of the picture, Finley and his partner could collect the entire ransom."

"I didn't hear either kidnapper mention April's name,"

Cassidy supplied, "but they did call someone. Maybe it was April. Is there any way to trace cell-phone activity out in that area?"

"Not usually, especially since the kidnappers would likely be using burners, as in disposable phones, but I'll look into it. Plus, we have a CSI team still combing the woods and the Tumbleweed. There's a chance they'll find some kind of evidence to prove who orchestrated the kidnappings and killed April."

Yeah, but that seemed a long shot. If there had been something obvious, the team would have already found it.

"We'll keep looking," Grayson assured him. "Keep going through the diary, too. Just stay put until you hear from me."

Sawyer ended the call, thankful that there hadn't been any bad news, but he wished there had been more progress in the investigation. Unless Finley started talking, this case could drag on longer than his and Cassidy's nerves could handle.

"You're stuck with me for a while," she said, setting aside her glass of tea.

True. And it might be more than just *a while*. There was no telling how many days—and nights—Cassidy and he would have to spend under the same roof. Of course, they had chaperones of sorts with the nanny-bodyguard and the two agents. But Sawyer was truly worried that chaperones weren't going to help him keep his hands off Cassidy.

In fact, nothing might help.

"Yes," she mumbled, pulling in her breath. That caused her chest to rise, just enough to capture his full attention.

"It'd make me dumber than dirt to act on this," he mumbled back.

And apparently that's exactly what he was. Dumber than dirt.

Sawyer ignored every red flag waving around him and leaned in and kissed her. He caught the little sound of surprise she made with the kiss. She made another of those sounds when he hooked his arm around her waist and snapped her to him.

Even though he knew he should stop, Sawyer just kept kissing her. Kept inching her closer and closer to him until Cassidy was pressed against him, body to body.

Yeah, there were plenty of memories, all right.

She tasted exactly as he remembered. Like something forbidden. Not far from the truth. She was in his protective custody, which made her hands off, but neither his hands nor the rest of him seemed interested in staying away from her.

Too bad Cassidy clearly felt the same way.

She didn't say so. Hard for her to speak through the deep kisses, but her body let him know this was exactly what she wanted. She wound her arms around his neck and kept kissing and touching so that the heat spiked through Sawyer.

His phone rang again, the sound shooting through the room and him. Once he tore himself away from Cassidy and her irresistible mouth, he was thankful for the reprieve. Until he saw the unknown-caller ID on the screen.

"Agent Ryland," Sawyer cautiously answered.

"You have to help me," the woman said, her words rushed together. It took him a moment to realize who the caller was.

"Dr. Blackwell? Where are you?" Sawyer asked, and he put the call on speaker so Cassidy could hear. "There are people looking for you."

"Please, you have to help me," she repeated. "Two men kidnapped me—"

And before the doctor could say another word, the line went dead.

Chapter Eleven

Cassidy's heart slammed against her chest. *No.* This couldn't be happening again. Even though she hardly knew Diane Blackwell, she did know what it was like to be taken captive. And in this case, the kidnappers were also killers.

Well, they were if it was the same people who'd taken April, Bennie and her.

Sawyer cursed, and he immediately scrolled through his numbers to call Grayson. No doubt so the sheriff could try to trace the call and locate the doctor before it was too late.

"Grayson," Sawyer said the moment he answered. "We've got a problem."

But before he could give the sheriff any details, Sawyer's phone beeped, indicating he had another call coming in. Cassidy glanced at the screen and saw unknown caller, the same as before.

"I'll have to get back to you," Sawyer said to Grayson, and he clicked over to the other call. "Diane?"

"It's me," the woman said in a whisper. It was hard to hear her words, but Cassidy had no trouble hearing the fear in her voice. "We got disconnected or something."

Better than the alternative of the kidnappers taking the phone. Or harming her so she couldn't speak.

"Where are you?" Sawyer asked. He took the landline phone off the hook, pressed in Grayson's number and handed it to Cassidy. "Tell him what's going on," Sawyer mouthed.

"I'm not sure where I am," the doctor answered. "Some kind of warehouse. I managed to get away from the men, and I stole one of their phones. But I know they're looking for me. That's why you have to help me."

Cassidy got through to Grayson and asked him to try to trace Diane's call. He kept her on hold while he tried to do that, and she gave Sawyer a nod to let him know what was happening.

"And I will help you," Sawyer assured her. "I'm having someone try to pinpoint your location now. Just stay on the line and describe where you are."

"A big metal building." Her breathing made a soft hiccupping sob. "It's empty except for some wooden crates."

"How'd you get there?" Sawyer pressed.

"The men were holding me in a nearby building. A vacant office." She paused, gave another of those panicky sobs. "I think I'm in San Antonio. Please, you have to help me."

"I will, I promise," Sawyer said. And Cassidy knew that he would certainly try. "Look around you. Can you see the city lights or hear traffic?"

"No. But the men didn't drive that long after they kidnapped me. God, I'm so scared."

"I know." Unlike Diane, Sawyer's voice was level and calm. But not the rest of him. He had a crushing grip on the phone. "Just give me all the details you can."

"Okay." But it still took her several long seconds to get control of her voice. "I'd just gotten back from Silver Creek and was in the parking lot of my office building. It's underground, and the light over my assigned space was broken or something." Another sob. "I didn't think anything of it, but the men took me the moment I stepped from my car."

Again, it was hard to hear. They'd done almost the same thing to her. Grabbed Cassidy as she was coming out of her downtown office. She'd left in a rush that day. Distracted. Because only moments earlier the kidnapper had called to tell her that they had her brother. The last thing Cassidy had expected was for them to kidnap her, too, and that she needed to get the money for the ransom.

"Did you see the men's faces or recognize them?" Sawyer demanded.

"No," the doctor answered, and didn't hesitate, either. "They wore these cartoon masks, like the kind kids wear to trick-or-treat. And they didn't speak. They just threw me on the floor of a van. There were no windows in the back, so I couldn't see where we were going."

"How long were you in the van?" Sawyer asked. "Because it can help me pinpoint where they took you."

"It's hard to think." Diane started to sob again.

"I know, but you can do this. You can help me save you."

It was silly, but Cassidy wished that she'd had him on the other end of the line when she'd been taken. She'd been out of her mind with fear for Bennie and for herself, and there had been no one like Sawyer to help. Still, he'd managed to save her, and she hoped he could do the same for Diane.

"The kidnappers drove for maybe fifteen minutes before they stopped and took me into the empty office," Diane finally said. "I ran here after I got away from the other building where they were holding me."

And she'd obviously hidden herself since the kidnappers hadn't found her all this time she'd been on the phone with Sawyer.

"Look around," Sawyer instructed, "and try to guess where you are."

"Uh." Diane made several more of those sounds and was, hopefully, looking around. "I think I'm on the south side of town near some abandoned buildings."

"Good." He motioned for Cassidy to relay that to Grayson, and she did. "Just try to remember if you saw something, anything that will help us find you."

"She's using a burner," Grayson said to Cassidy, and she passed that information on to Sawyer.

Cassidy had already learned that the cops couldn't trace a disposable cell, and that meant it was even more critical for Diane to tell them exactly where she was.

"Put my call on Speaker," Grayson added to her, "so Diane and Sawyer can hear this."

Cassidy did, and she held the landline phone near Sawyer's cell.

"San Antonio P.D. is sending two cruisers out to an area on the south side where there are warehouses," Grayson explained. "Diane, I need you to listen for the sirens. That'll help us pinpoint your location."

"Wait," Diane said, her voice shaking again. "I think the men are coming into the building. Oh, God. I think I hear footsteps."

Cassidy put her fingers to her mouth. Held her breath.

"Just stay quiet a moment and try to keep out of sight." It was good advice, but Sawyer mouthed some profanity after giving it. Probably because he hated not being able to help her. Diane was alone and no doubt terrified.

The seconds crawled by, and even though Diane wasn't saying anything, Cassidy could hear plenty from Grayson. Speaking in whispers now, he was giving instructions to the officers heading out to look for the woman. She only hoped that the cops got to Diane before the kidnappers found her.

"I think they're gone," Diane finally continued. Some relief was in her voice, still mixed with fear. "I remembered something else while I was waiting. There was a driver's license clipped to the visor in the van, and I saw the man's name. Joe Finley."

Cassidy seriously doubted it was a coincidence that the surname matched the kidnapper they already had in custody, and several moments after she gave the name to Grayson, he confirmed it.

"Joe and Chester are brothers," Grayson explained. She heard the click of computer keys. "And like Chester, he has a long criminal record. He has a fondness for working as hired muscle for loan sharks."

And these were almost certainly the men who'd held Bennie and her. Men with violent criminal records, and now they had Diane.

"Why?" Cassidy hadn't meant to say that aloud, but it grabbed Sawyer's attention. He nodded, repeated it.

"Why would these men take you, Diane?" Sawyer came out and asked.

"I don't know." Diane's breath broke again, and there was another sob. "Maybe because they think I know something about April. Something that will incriminate them in her murder."

That was a good guess, and it might all lead back to April's therapy sessions with the doctor. Or the diary. "Did April ever say anything about the Finleys?" Cassidy asked.

"Nothing that I remember. She mainly talked about Willy and how terrified she was of him."

Sawyer's gaze met hers, and Cassidy could see the

same conclusion in his eyes. Had Willy hired the brothers to kidnap Bennie, April and her?

And now Dr. Blackwell?

Willy could have wanted Bennie and her for the ransom, but he could have had the doctor kidnapped to silence her.

Or for another reason.

"According to April's diary, she thought you and Bennie were having an affair," Sawyer said. "Maybe the Finleys took you in the hopes of still getting the ransom from Bennie and Cassidy."

"No," Diane practically shouted. Then she repeated it in a much lower voice. "I'm not having an affair with Bennie. Never have, never will. April was paranoid that way, always believing that her lovers were cheating on her with someone else."

"But why did she think Bennie was cheating on her with you?" Cassidy asked.

"Who knows. The woman wasn't mentally stable. Wait, I remember something else," Diane said. "I heard this Joe Finley mention a debt that Bennie owes."

Cassidy's heart felt as if it skipped a beat. "Joe said Bennie owed him money?"

"No, only that Bennie was in debt," Diane clarified. "Why, do you know anything about that?"

This time when Sawyer's gaze came to hers, Cassidy saw the questions. And maybe some distrust. After all, she had already admitted that she would do pretty much anything to save her kid brother, and he might be thinking she was withholding something.

And she was. Though not intentionally.

"Bennie did owe some money," Cassidy admitted. "But I don't know the details. A couple of days before we were kidnapped, Bennie asked me for money to pay off some loan. But I refused. I wanted more information, and he wouldn't give it to me. So I told him he'd have to wait until the first of the month when he got his allowance from his trust fund."

Too bad they'd been kidnapped before then.

Cassidy shook her head, looked at Sawyer. "I swear, I forgot all about it until just now. Besides, it might not have anything to do with what Joe said."

But that felt and sounded like an excuse, the same kind of outs she'd been giving her brother most of his life. The odds were that this was indeed connected to the kidnappings.

"Oh, mercy," Cassidy mumbled. "They might have kidnapped us because of what Bennie owed them."

Sawyer looked up at the ceiling, added some profanity under his breath. "And if so, then there'll likely be a ransom demand for you, Diane. They probably think your husband will pay to get you released."

"He would," she immediately agreed. "If he knew my life was on the line, he'd pay, and that means these kidnappers won't stop looking for me...." Diane's words trailed off, and for several seconds, all Cassidy could hear was the woman's suddenly heavy breathing. "I hear sirens. They're in the distance, but I can hear them."

"Good," Grayson answered. "When the sirens get closer, let us know."

"Oh, God," Diane said. "I heard the kidnappers again, too. I think they just came into the warehouse. I'll text you when the sirens are closer."

And with that, she ended the call.

"She hung up," Sawyer relayed to Grayson.

"Let me know when she calls back," Grayson said.

Sawyer assured him that they would, and he turned

to Cassidy. "Tell me everything about this money that Bennie owes."

She was shaking her head before he'd fully asked the question. Except he didn't just ask. He gave her a law-man's order.

"I've already told you everything I know," Cassidy insisted. "But I know where to get answers."

Since she didn't have her cell with her, she used the house phone to call her brother. Bennie answered on the first ring, and she put the call on speaker.

"What happened?" Bennie snapped, clearly on edge. "What's wrong?"

Cassidy had a quick debate about how much to tell him and decided to focus on the money for now. There was no need to give the details of Diane's abduction.

"Before we were kidnapped, you said you needed cash to pay off a loan. Who did you owe money?" she asked.

He made a huffing sound of surprise. "There's a kid-napper still on the loose, and that's what you want to talk about?"

Now Cassidy huffed. She knew her brother well enough to know when he was stonewalling her. "Yes, it's what I want to talk about. Tell me about that loan."

Bennie mumbled something she didn't catch, and he hesitated so long that she wasn't sure he would answer. "You wouldn't recognize the man's name," Bennie finally said, "but he owns several bars. He loaned me some money to cover my gambling debts."

She looked at Sawyer, expecting to see an I-told-you-so expression, but he only scowled. "How much did you borrow?" Sawyer pressed.

Again, a long hesitation. "A quarter of a million."

Oh, mercy. Six months of his allowance wouldn't

have covered that. "Was this bar owner pressing you to pay him?"

"Yes, and that's why I asked you for the money. I shouldn't have to remind you that you refused." Bennie made it sound as if this was somehow her fault.

It wasn't. And even though this wasn't the time to have a long talk with her brother, she still had some things to clear up.

"Were we kidnapped because of the money you owe?" Cassidy came out and asked.

"No." There was zero hesitation this time. "How could you even ask that? I wouldn't have put you in that kind of danger."

Cassidy desperately wanted to believe him, but she wasn't so sure. "Then why were we taken?"

"Probably for the money that you were going to pay the kidnappers for our release. Maybe money, too, from Sawyer for the baby if it turned out to be his. I think April could have set it up. She's a gold digger, you know. Or maybe it was that psycho Willy."

Both of them were good suspects, but April was dead, and Willy was pointing the finger at Bennie. Cassidy wasn't sure who to believe.

"One more thing. Were you involved with Dr. Diane Blackwell?" she asked.

"What? No." Another quick answer. "Why, is that what she said?"

"April did, in her diary."

"Well, April was lying." Bennie cursed and then made a sound of frustration. "Hell's bells, Cassidy, why would you believe her over me?" However, he didn't wait for an answer. "April was angry because I ended things with her. She would have said anything to get back at me."

"But why this?" Cassidy continued. "How would saying you're involved with Diane get back at you?"

"Because it would have made it seem as if I was trying to manipulate April's therapy by sleeping with her shrink. April could have probably used that to get herself moved to another doctor. She hated Diane."

From all accounts, that was true. Of course, most of the information Cassidy had on that subject had come from Willy, a man she didn't trust.

"I have to go," her brother said, his voice edged with anger. "My pain meds are kicking in, and I'm getting sleepy. I suggest before you call me again with accusations, you get your facts straight first."

"Facts are exactly what I want to get straight," Sawyer said. "Come to the Silver Creek sheriff's office tomorrow morning so you can answer some more questions."

That brought on some more profanity, but Bennie issued a terse, "Fine. See you then."

Bennie hung up, leaving Cassidy to stand there and stare at the phone. A dozen emotions were going through her, but first and foremost was anger. Bennie might truly have had something to do with the kidnapping.

"I'm sorry," Sawyer said.

No scowl or glare. He was staring at her now, and all those previous emotions had been replaced with sympathy.

"How can I find out if Bennie had a connection to the Finley brothers?" Even though it hurt just to ask the question, Cassidy had to know.

"I can call my cousin Kade. He's FBI, too, and he'll be able to check Bennie's phone records." Sawyer waited until she gave him the nod before he took the house phone from her and made the call.

The part of her that had spent years protecting her

brother hated that this had to be done, but she had to know the truth. Especially since April was dead, possibly because of the failed kidnapping attempt.

Sawyer finished his call with Kade, hung up the phone and pulled Cassidy to him. It wasn't the heated kissing session like before. He held her for what turned out to be a few precious seconds before his phone rang again.

Cassidy glanced at the screen, expecting to see the unknown-caller ID that had popped up before. But it was Nate Ryland's name, instead. She'd never met him but knew he was Sawyer's cousin and that he was a lieutenant with the San Antonio P.D. She held her breath, hoping the cops had managed to find Diane and that she'd been rescued.

"Well?" Sawyer greeted the moment he answered.

"We spotted the two kidnappers running from one of the warehouses," Nate started. "They got away. So we went inside, but the place was empty."

"Maybe Diane got out ahead of the kidnappers?" Sawyer suggested.

"Maybe." Nate paused, a long time. "But it doesn't look good. The phone she was using is here. Crushed to bits. Some of the crates have been turned over. Looks like there was a struggle."

Sawyer cursed. "Any sign of Diane?"

"None. But there's blood on the floor."

Chapter Twelve

Sawyer stared at the photos of the warehouse. The top-pled crates. The crushed phone.

And the blood.

Since it had been more than twelve hours since they'd last heard from Diane, Sawyer figured one of two things had happened. The kidnappers had injured her when they'd taken her captive again. Or it was worse than that.

Maybe they had killed her.

They already had one unsolved murder on their hands, and he hated that they might have another. Especially when those murders could be connected right back to Cassidy, Emma and him.

Cassidy finished her phone call and peered at him from over the top of a coffee mug that Grayson had scrounged up for her. "The nanny said Emma was fine."

Good. That was something at least.

Sawyer had hated to leave the baby, but she was in good hands with the nanny-bodyguard and the two agents. He wished he could say the same for Cassidy. Sawyer had wanted her to stay at the safe house, too, while he drove into town to question her brother. But she had insisted on coming along.

And he couldn't blame her.

If it were his brother in the hot seat, Sawyer would have done the same. The trouble was, he wasn't sure Cassidy could handle much more stress, and here he was about to add what would be a tense interrogation.

He heard the footsteps in the hall, and seconds later his cousin Mason appeared in the doorway. "Just got the test results back. It was Diane's blood in the warehouse."

Even though it was exactly what Sawyer had expected, he still cursed. He'd held out some hope that the woman had managed to injure one of her kidnappers, but no such luck.

"It's not much blood," Mason went on. "Not nearly enough to indicate a fatal wound."

No, but they both knew she could have been taken elsewhere to bleed out.

"Kade faxed this to you," Mason added, dropping several pages onto the desk that Sawyer was using as his makeshift office. "Bennie's phone records." And he shot Cassidy a look that almost seemed to say *brace yourself* before he strolled away.

The phone records got Cassidy's attention, because she hurried around to his side of the desk. "Rex Ross," Sawyer said when he saw the name. According to the note Kade had made, Ross was the bar owner who Bennie had mentioned the night before. The one he owed money to.

"Bennie called him at least a dozen times," Cassidy pointed out. Looking over his shoulder, she leaned closer. Too close. Until her breasts touched his back. "Sorry," she mumbled.

Sawyer looked up at her. "If we start apologizing for every little touch, we're not going to be doing much else than saying I'm sorry."

Of course, that didn't stop him from reacting to that accidental touch. And despite everything else going on, he was reminded again of the heat. Reminded too of the stupid kissing session. Stupid because he'd done it and equally stupid because he wanted to do it again.

Sawyer was still trying to push those kissing thoughts aside when he saw Cassidy's eyes widen. He followed her gaze to another name on the list.

Chester Finley.

Cassidy made a soft gasp and put her hand over her throat. "Why would Bennie have contacted him?"

"It was an incoming call," Sawyer pointed out. "Made about four days ago. It doesn't look as if Bennie answered it." Still, it didn't answer the question of why Chester had called Bennie in the first place.

Cassidy stepped away, and he could see her fighting to hang on to her composure. Fighting to make sense of this, too. "Chester was on that landscaping crew," she said. "So maybe he called Bennie under the pretense of that, when he really wanted to get some information that would help him with the kidnapping."

That was a good theory, but if he wanted to give Bennie the benefit of the doubt—and he would for Cassidy's sake—then Sawyer could see a different angle. "Chester might have called Bennie to make him look guilty of participating in the kidnappings. It could have all been a setup."

Cassidy thought about that a moment. Nodded. And looked way more relieved than she should have. It was a thin theory at best. Especially when Sawyer turned to the second page of calls. Again, one name immediately snagged his attention.

Dr. Diane Blackwell.

There were at least a dozen calls, both incoming and outgoing, and unlike the unanswered one from Chester,

Bennie had most definitely answered these. Some of the phone conversations had lasted more than a half hour.

Funny that neither Diane nor Bennie had mentioned it.

Did that mean April's allegations were true, that Bennie had indeed had an affair with Diane? And if he had, then why the heck had he denied it? Bennie already looked guilty enough without adding lies that could easily be traced.

Sawyer took out his phone and called Grayson, who was working from home. "What's the latest on Chester Finley?" Because if Bennie and Diane weren't offering up the truth, maybe Chester would.

"He's still not answering questions, but he said if we could prove his brother was safe, then he'd cooperate."

Interesting. And Sawyer wasn't sure what to make of it. "Is Chester worried the cops will find and kill his brother, or is this about something else? Maybe Chester doesn't trust the other kidnapper involved?"

"Sounds that way to me. We're beefing up our efforts to find Diane and his brother. Once we have Joe in custody, I figure Chester will try to work out a plea deal to save his brother and his own butt."

That would be a best-case scenario—the brothers talking and handing over the person who'd orchestrated all of this. And Sawyer didn't think either Chester or his brother had been the mastermind. No, they weren't the sort for that. They were hired muscle, and that meant someone had done the hiring.

Sawyer was about to ask Grayson if there were any other updates, but he heard the bell jangle over the front door. Cassidy peered out from the door.

"It's Bennie," she said softly.

There was plenty of dread in her voice, and Sawyer knew how she felt. Even though he'd investigated Bennie with the hopes of making an arrest, he was no longer that anxious to put Cassidy's brother behind bars.

Another side effect of that kissing session.

And his feelings for her.

Yeah, he had them, all right, and they'd come at a damn inconvenient time. He'd lost his objectivity. His focus. Heck, maybe his mind.

Cassidy stared at him. "You look angry."

"I am," Sawyer admitted, and he gathered up the phone records and stepped around her so he could face Bennie. Her brother didn't look any happier to see Sawyer than Sawyer was to see him.

For that matter, neither did Cassidy.

She certainly didn't go to her brother and hug him as she'd done the last time Bennie had arrived at the sheriff's office. And that was a little surprising, considering that Bennie's face still showed the bruises and cuts he'd gotten while being held captive.

Well, a theoretical captive anyway.

With everything they'd learned, Sawyer had to accept that Bennie might have orchestrated the whole thing. If so, Sawyer wasn't sure he could stop himself from adding more cuts and bruises to Bennie's face. After all, the kidnapping could have gotten Cassidy killed.

"This way," Sawyer told Bennie, and he hitched his thumb toward one of the interview rooms.

"I don't know why I had to come back to this place," Bennie complained, but he followed Cassidy and Sawyer into the room.

Sawyer was about to insist that Cassidy stay out of this, but Bennie's whole lack of concern for her reared its ugly head. If Bennie was guilty, she needed to hear it from her brother's own mouth. Then Sawyer could turn him over to one of his cousins so they could do the official interrogation.

And maybe make an arrest.

"There's no need for you to worry about my debts," Bennie went on, his attention fastened to Cassidy. "I've been in touch with the bar owner and worked out a payment plan."

"With Rex Ross," Sawyer provided.

Bennie flinched. Then his mouth tightened. "You've been spying on me?"

"No, but we have been going through your phone records." Sawyer dropped the pages on the table in front of them.

One look at them and Bennie slowly sank into the chair. "You saw the calls I made to Diane." He spoke to Cassidy not to Sawyer.

"You said you weren't having an affair with her," Cassidy reminded him.

"And I wasn't." Even though he'd only been seated for a few seconds, Bennie sprang to his feet. "What— do you believe him now over me?" In this case, the *him* was Sawyer, and Bennie stabbed his stiff index finger in his direction.

Cassidy didn't jump to assure him. She folded her arms over her chest. "I'm merely asking—are you having an affair with Diane?"

"No," Bennie howled. "Of course not. She was a married woman, and I wouldn't have wanted to risk making enemies with her husband even if they are separated."

"Then why call her?" Cassidy demanded.

"Diane wanted to discuss April, that's all. She wanted some insight into April's past because she thought that might help with her therapy."

While that explanation sounded a little unconventional, Sawyer couldn't dispute it. Well, not until he'd spoken to Diane anyway. Hopefully, the doctor was still alive and he'd be able to do just that.

"Why would Diane think you have insight into April?" Sawyer asked. "You hadn't known her that long."

Bennie lifted his shoulder, and his mouth settled into a pout, making him look like a kid. "I guess April talked about me a lot during their sessions. Mostly lies, I'm sure. She had a hard time telling the truth about anything."

Still, April had convinced her shrink that Bennie had information that would help her recovery. Sawyer wasn't sure he could buy that, but he moved on to the next subject.

He tapped the next name of interest. Chester Finley. "Why would he call you just days before the kidnapping?"

Bennie stared at it a moment. "I have no idea. I saw his name on my caller ID, didn't recognize it, so I didn't answer it. That number belonged to Chester Finley?"

Sawyer nodded and looked for any sign that Bennie was lying. He didn't seem to be, but Sawyer reminded himself that Bennie had a lot of nasty habits, and that included breaking the law. He probably wouldn't have any trouble lying to an FBI agent.

Bennie shook his head, huffed. "If I had any idea Finley was on the verge of kidnapping Cassidy and me, I would have taken the call and tried to talk him out of it."

If that was true, Bennie would have almost certainly failed. There was too much money at stake for Chester and Joe to back off. But the question was—did the men have help from Bennie?

"You don't believe me," Bennie said, his nostrils flaring now. "Well, the person you should be looking at is Diane. I think April was right to be afraid of the doctor.

Have you considered that Diane could be behind the kidnappings? A million dollars is a lot of motive, and Diane could have manipulated April into helping her."

Yes, Sawyer had considered it, along with a lot of other angles. Still, it was one he shouldn't continue to dismiss just because Bennie had reminded him of it.

Sawyer fired off a text to Kade and asked his cousin to check Diane's financial records. He wasn't sure just how deep Kade could dig, but maybe they could learn if Diane had any money problems.

Like Bennie did.

"Talk to me about this payment plan you have for your loan to Rex Ross," Sawyer insisted.

"Nothing to talk about. Rex has agreed to let me pay him monthly from my trust-fund allowance."

No way did that sound right to Sawyer. "Really? Bookies aren't usually that accommodating."

"Well, in this case the arrangement works in his favor. Until the debt's paid off, Rex gets paid most of my trust fund, and he's added a hefty amount of interest. I guess the profit he'll be making was enough to make him agree to the payments."

Cassidy huffed, put her hands on the table and leaned in until she was right in her brother's face. "If that's a lie or if there's something you're keeping from me, now is the time to tell me."

Bennie's eyes instantly narrowed, and he stood, slowly, without taking his gaze from his sister. "It's clear whose side you're on. What, are you sleeping with Sawyer again?"

"That's none of your business," Cassidy snapped before Sawyer could say anything. "Now, what are you keeping from me?"

"Nothing," he said through clenched teeth.

Bennie didn't get a chance to add more because the jangling sound got everyone's attention. The sound meant they had a visitor, and while that wasn't at all unusual in the sheriff's office, Sawyer didn't want a kidnapper storming the place.

But it wasn't a kidnapper.

Well, maybe it wasn't.

Willy walked in, and his gaze went straight to the hall where Sawyer was now standing. "I found out something about Dr. Blackwell."

Until Willy said that, Sawyer had been about to tell him to take a hike, but that stopped him. "What?" Sawyer snapped, walking closer.

But Sawyer wasn't walking alone. He heard footsteps behind him, glanced over his shoulder and there was Cassidy and Bennie. The stay-put glare he shot them didn't even make them pause.

Willy opened his mouth but then closed it when he spotted Bennie. "He'd better not be here to accuse me of anything."

"If the shoes fits…" Bennie grumbled. Obviously, there was no love lost between the two.

"What'd you find out about Diane?" Sawyer pressed, ignoring the sharp looks Bennie and Willy were doling out to each other.

"I heard a lot of talk about Diane being strapped for cash because her hubby cut her off without a dime," Willy continued. "I've also heard that she's within weeks of losing her home and business because she's got an expensive drug habit that she wants to keep hidden. I figure that gives her motive to team up with Bennie here to put together his own kidnapping."

Bennie cursed. "I'm sick and tired of people accusing me of things I didn't do."

"Join the club," Willy grumbled. "The only reason I'm here is to show Agent Ryland that there are folks with a bigger motive than me for these kidnappings. And April's murder."

"But you have a motive, too," Sawyer reminded him. "You were jealous of April because she'd broken things off with you. That's a big motive, if you ask me. Besides, why would Bennie and Diane want April dead?"

Willy casually lifted his shoulder as if he wasn't affected by the accusation Sawyer had just tossed at him. "Maybe Bennie wanted April dead because she was a loose end. If she knew about the kidnapping, was maybe even a part of it, then the poor rich boy here wouldn't have wanted her hanging around to rat on him. It's the same for Diane."

"If she's alive," Sawyer replied, and he volleyed glances between both Willy and Bennie. Both men seemed surprised that she might be dead.

Seemed.

"Maybe Diane is a loose end, too," Sawyer added. "Because she's missing, and there are signs of foul play."

There were just a few seconds of silence before both men started to declare their innocence. And maybe they were. But Sawyer kept pressing. "Where were you both last night?"

"At home," Bennie immediately answered. "With a deputy guard at my front door. If I'd left, he would have known about it."

Not necessarily. The O'Neal estate was huge, and Bennie could have slipped out.

The phone rang, and even though there was no dispatcher or receptionist out front today, Grayson or one of the deputies must have answered it because it stopped after just two rings.

"And what about you?" Sawyer asked Willy. "Where were you last night?"

"I was at home, too. Alone. I didn't figure I'd need to have an alibi for every minute of my life."

Sawyer gave him a flat look. "Well, you figured wrong. I'll check your phone records to see if you're telling the truth."

That pretty much drained the color from Willy's face, but the man didn't get a chance to change his story or balk again about his innocence. Grayson stepped out from his office, and he motioned for Sawyer to come closer, which he did, bringing Cassidy along with him. But Sawyer motioned for Willy and Bennie to stay put.

"What's wrong?" Sawyer asked after noticing Grayson's concerned expression.

"It's someone from the lab." Grayson handed Sawyer the phone. "They just got back the results of the baby's DNA test."

Chapter Thirteen

Cassidy held her breath and watched Sawyer as he took the phone from Grayson. He didn't put the call on Speaker, probably because Willy and Bennie were still there, and she couldn't tell from Sawyer's expression what the person from the lab was saying to him. She could only stand there and wait to see whose baby had been put in the middle of this dangerous mix.

The cops didn't have DNA from Monica Barnes, but they had Sawyer's. If he was Emma's father, then Monica was almost certainly the little girl's mother.

And maybe the kidnappers had known that all along.

It would explain why they'd had her take the child to Sawyer and get that photo. The proof that would have made him pay any amount of ransom.

But she had to stop and shake her head.

The kidnappers had told her to leave the baby with Sawyer and bring back the photo. Why? If they'd just held on to the baby, then they could have collected more money.

So, what was this about?

Ruining Sawyer's reputation by uncovering his involvement with a cocktail waitress? That would hardly ruin him unless the person behind this wanted to somehow tie him to the kidnappings.

And that brought her back to her brother.

Of their suspects, Bennie was the only one who would want revenge on Sawyer. It all went back to that investigation a year ago and Sawyer's attempt to arrest Bennie.

Mercy, had her brother decided to get even by embroiling Sawyer in a kidnapping? If so, she prayed she could deal with the consequence.

"Yes, run it," Sawyer said to the person on the other end of the line. He clicked End Call, turned and immediately snared her gaze. "April is Emma's biological mother."

The relief washed through her. For a few seconds anyway. And then she realized what this meant. Emma wasn't Sawyer's child, and he had no claim to her. Yes, Sawyer and she had only had the baby for a short period of time, but Cassidy felt the loss.

Apparently, Sawyer did, too, because that wasn't happiness she saw in his eyes.

"Who's the kid's father?" Willy snapped.

The man's eyes were easy to read, too. The anger had returned with a vengeance. No doubt because they already knew that Emma wasn't Willy's, and that meant April had indeed cheated on him.

Sawyer shook his head. "We don't know."

"Maybe I'm looking at him." Willy glared at Sawyer.

"I already told you that I never even met April."

Willy's glare got worse. "Prove it. Or prove to me the test isn't fake."

"It's not fake," Sawyer insisted.

But judging from the sound Willy made, he obviously didn't agree. "For all I know, you could be covering up your guilt in all of this. Where were you last night?" Willy added, repeating the question Sawyer had asked him earlier.

But Sawyer didn't respond to that. He turned to Grayson instead. "I was never with April, so there's no chance Emma could be mine, but I told the lab tech to go ahead and compare her DNA to mine. To exclude me so we can focus on finding the real father. Maybe April's killer, too."

Sawyer's gaze landed on Bennie. "My DNA's already in the system at Quantico, but since you've never been arrested for a felony, yours isn't. I want you to give us a sample of your DNA so we can run it against Emma's."

When Bennie didn't respond, Cassidy reeled in his direction. "Please tell me you're not going to argue about this, too?" she said.

Oh, her brother didn't like that. "All right," Bennie finally said, and he repeated it in a much louder, firmer voice when Cassidy continued to stare at him.

Had Bennie hesitated for a reason?

He'd already said the child wasn't his, so there should have been no hesitation in giving them a sample of his DNA. Besides, Bennie had to have known this would happen. If neither Willy nor Sawyer was the baby's father, then the next likely person was her brother. Well, the next likely person in the room anyway. It was entirely possible that April had had lovers none of them knew about.

Grayson disappeared into another room, and a few seconds later, he came back with a plastic bag that contained a swab. "Use it on the inside of your mouth," Grayson instructed.

Bennie took the test kit, stared at it, before his gaze came back to hers. "The cops and FBI set people up all the time. You know Sawyer has it in for me."

It took her a moment to tamp down the anger so she could speak. "No, I don't know that. Because Sawyer wouldn't set you up."

"Yeah, you say that because you have a thing for him, but I don't trust him."

Sawyer hitched his thumb at Grayson. "The sheriff will send your DNA sample to the lab. Unless you think Cassidy's got a thing for him, too."

"No." Her brother dragged that out a few syllables. "But you and the sheriff are cousins."

Sawyer huffed. "What possible reason would we have to falsify DNA evidence?" He didn't wait for Bennie to respond. "Emma's mother is dead, and we need to find her father. Not a fake one. But the real one so he can have a say in her future."

That hurt, too. It was stupid to have gotten this attached to Emma. After all, there had been no guarantees that Sawyer was her father. Now, Emma's father would come and take her. Give her a real name. And Cassidy might never see her again.

"Do the test," Willy demanded.

Her brother turned as if to blast Willy to smithereens, but Sawyer stepped between them.

"Just do the test," Sawyer repeated to Bennie.

But Bennie still stared at the bag. "Swear to me that you won't use this to set me up for April's murder."

The muscles in Sawyer's jaw stirred. "I swear." Though she wasn't sure how he could speak with his teeth clenched like that.

Bennie finally opened the bag and scrubbed the swab inside his mouth. As if he'd declared war on it, he crammed the swab back in the bag and tossed it to Grayson.

"Satisfied?" Bennie snarled, and the snarl was aimed at her.

"Yes. Thank you." She hated this tension between Bennie and her, but it couldn't be helped. She trusted Sawyer and his cousin to do the right thing. They wouldn't tamper with the test, and soon Bennie would be excluded as Emma's father.

And that would take them back to square one as far as the baby was concerned.

Cassidy almost hated to ask, but she had to know. "Did the lab try to match Emma's DNA with people already in the system?"

In other words—criminals.

With April's shady past, it wasn't much of a stretch to believe that she'd had an affair with a criminal. And that might make things tricky when it came to Emma's *future*.

"The lab's running that now." Sawyer touched her arm, rubbed gently. "They'll let us know if they get a match." And he sounded as troubled by that as she was.

Cassidy heard her brother mumble some profanity, and when she looked in his direction, she realized he hadn't missed Sawyer's arm rub. It no doubt caused Bennie to believe that Sawyer and she were sleeping together again.

Willy laughed. He obviously hadn't missed it, either. "Bennie, I almost feel sorry for you. *Almost*. I figure by this time tomorrow, one of these Rylands will be arresting you for murder. And you know what? I can't wait. Somebody's gonna pay for killing April, and I have a good feeling it's gonna be you."

Willy's phone rang, the music from his ringtone way too perky for the tension in the room, and he glanced down at the screen. His eyes widened, and he made a slight sound of surprise. "Gotta go," he mumbled, and as he pressed the button to take the call, he walked out of the building.

Sawyer stared at Willy on the other side of the reinforced glass.

"Don't worry," Grayson said. "We'll keep an eye on

him. And I'll call you the moment the lab has anything. Go ahead and get Cassidy out of here."

"You mean, take her back to the safe house," Bennie said with the same disdain he'd used discussing the DNA sample.

Her brother stared at that sample in Grayson's possession and cursed under his breath. "I have to talk to you," Bennie said to Cassidy. "In private."

No. Cassidy didn't like the sound of that, and she didn't like Sawyer's reaction, either. He was shaking his head before Bennie finished.

"She's not going anywhere with you," Sawyer insisted. "You're a suspect in her kidnapping."

Even though Bennie already knew that, she saw the temper flare in his eyes. "I wouldn't hurt my sister," he insisted. And he waited as if he expected her to jump to defend him.

Normally, she would have done just that, but Cassidy was too weary—and too troubled—to do it today. Besides, right now it wasn't safe to go anywhere with anyone other than Sawyer.

Grayson excused himself, saying something about having a courier pick up Bennie's DNA sample, and disappeared into his office. Bennie stayed as if waiting for Sawyer to do the same, but he didn't move.

"This is a private discussion," Bennie argued. "It's between me and my sister." But he stopped, stared at her. Cursed again. "Whatever I tell you, you'll just repeat to him, won't you?"

She nodded. "If it pertains to this investigation." And she prayed it didn't, but one look at Bennie's body language, and Cassidy could only groan.

Yes, it did pertain to the investigation.

"Tell me," Cassidy ordered.

Her brother shook his head. Mumbled something. Dodged her gaze. "Am I free to go?" Bennie asked Sawyer. Not a troubled tone and expression, just furious.

Cassidy was sure she was the cause of a lot of that fury. But she wasn't backing down. Bennie had something to say, and he was going to say it—even if it got him arrested.

"What did you need to tell me?" she demanded.

Even though Bennie had been the one to insist on this discussion, it still took him several moments to get started. "I did have an affair with April."

Sweet heaven. There it was, all spelled out. Bennie's motive for murder.

"That's not exactly a news flash," Sawyer said under his breath.

Bennie cursed, looked away. "And the timing is right, so the baby could possibly be mine. *Possibly*," he repeated.

Now it was Cassidy who wanted to curse. "So, you lied to us earlier when you denied it."

"Yeah, I lied," he readily admitted. "Because it was a private matter between April and me."

Cassidy's mouth nearly dropped open. "This is a murder investigation and therefore no longer a private matter." She groaned and stepped away from Bennie when he reached to take hold of her arm.

It sickened her to think of the lies he'd told. Lies that could cause Sawyer to bring charges against him. Of course, there was something more important in all of this.

Emma.

If she was indeed Bennie's daughter, then he would have a claim to her. Cassidy still loved her brother, but he was nowhere near responsible enough to raise a child. However, there was a silver lining in all of this. If Bennie was the father, then maybe that would mean Cassidy would have an easier time getting custody of the little girl.

If that's what she wanted to do.

And she realized she did.

Except it was more than that. Her stupid mind had been weaving a fantasy of Sawyer, her and Emma. A fantasy that she was certain Sawyer didn't share, even though it was obvious he cared for the baby. Of course, he might not care for her so much now if it turned out that Emma had Bennie's blood.

She glanced at Sawyer to see if he, too, was thinking of Emma, but he had his attention nailed to Bennie. "No more lies," Sawyer warned him. "Did you kill April?"

"No," Bennie snapped. And he repeated it when he glanced at both of them. "I had no reason to want her dead."

"Really?" Sawyer said with a boatload of sarcasm. "From what we're learning, April was mentally unstable and a gold digger. I'm betting she didn't take it calmly when you tried to end things with her."

"She didn't," Bennie admitted under his breath. His gaze fired to Sawyer again. "But that doesn't mean I killed her. I figured eventually she'd find someone else and move on."

"Hard to move on when she was pregnant," Cassidy pointed out.

"Yeah." And that's all Bennie said for several moments. "But I didn't believe her when she said the baby was mine. I thought it was just her way of hanging on to me."

Cassidy huffed. "For Pete's sake, you were sleeping with her. You must have at least considered that Emma could be yours. Why didn't you offer to help out, maybe pay April's medical bills? If you'd come to me with that, I would have helped you."

Bennie shook his head. "I needed your help with those loans from Rex Ross. I figured April had her own sources to pay the bills."

Cassidy wanted to scream at his sheer selfishness. Wanted to scream at herself, too, since she'd helped to make him this way by always getting him out of trouble. Well, that ended today.

She got right in his face. "If Emma is yours, you *will* do the right thing for her, even if it means giving her up. And if there are criminal charges, you'll face those, too."

Bennie didn't argue, but he did look as if she'd slapped him. "Am I free to go?" he repeated to Sawyer.

Sawyer didn't jump to answer that, but he eventually nodded. "Don't leave town." That was likely the best he could do since he couldn't arrest Bennie without evidence.

Cassidy watched her brother skulk away, leaving through the front door. Only then did she realize Willy wasn't out there any longer. She hadn't noticed him leaving, and she wondered just how much of their conversation he'd heard.

"I'm sorry," Sawyer said. He slipped his arm around her.

Cassidy was about to tell him that she was okay, that she didn't need him to hold her. But she quickly realized she was wrong. She was trembling. And furious. And terrified that her brother might have indeed murdered the mother of his own child. If so, that made him the worst kind of monster.

The tears came, and she swiped them away, hoping they wouldn't return. But they did.

"Come on," Sawyer whispered. "Let's head back to the safe house."

She didn't resist when he started leading her down the hall, though it would take them an hour or more to get back to the house. That's because Sawyer wouldn't take the direct route, and he would have to drive around first to make sure no one was following them. It would mean a lot of time in his truck while she was on the verge of falling apart. Still, if anyone could help her through this, it was Sawyer.

Cassidy cringed at that thought.

She shouldn't be leaning on him like this. Shouldn't be taking comfort in his arms. Because that could only lead to a broken heart.

Sawyer led her to the back door and the parking lot where he'd left the truck. But the moment he opened the door, he immediately stepped in front of her and drew his gun.

That put her heart in her throat, and Cassidy peered over his shoulder to see what had caused Sawyer to react that way.

It was Willy.

He was still talking on the phone and was pacing across the small parking lot. Willy stopped both the pacing and talking when he saw Sawyer's gun.

"I might have a lead on Diane," Willy said, putting his hand over the phone.

"Call me with it," Sawyer snapped. Without taking his attention off Willy, he reached inside the door and took one of the keys off a peg on the wall. "Grayson, I need to use your SUV. My truck might have been compromised."

Oh, mercy. She hadn't even considered that, but she was glad Sawyer had. Willy could have put some kind of tracking device on the truck so the kidnappers could find the location of the safe house.

"I'll check it after you're gone," Grayson assured him, and he joined them in the doorway.

"No need to draw your guns," Willy snarled. "I'm just trying to help you."

"Thanks," Sawyer snarled back. "But right now, you can help us by leaving. You're making my trigger finger itch."

Willy didn't seem particularly concerned about that. But he was angry. Maybe because of the gun. However, he kept glancing down at the phone, and he continued to do that even as he was leaving.

Sawyer waited several minutes before he stepped out. "Cassidy, stay here with Grayson," he insisted.

With his gun still drawn, he fired glances all around before he used the keypad to unlock Grayson's black SUV that was parked on the side of the building. If Willy or someone had indeed managed to plant a tracking device onto the truck, maybe they hadn't done that to the other vehicle, as well.

When Sawyer reached the SUV, he stooped down and looked beneath it. Not just in one place but all around the vehicle. He unlocked it and opened the passenger's-side door before he motioned for her to come out of the building.

Cassidy did, and she didn't dawdle. She hurried to the SUV, and the moment she reached Sawyer, he helped her onto the seat.

There was some movement from the corner of her eye. Sawyer saw it, too, because he whipped in that direction. But it was Willy, still talking on the phone, this time while he paced on the sidewalk in front of the sheriff's office.

Even though Willy didn't appear to be paying any attention to them, Sawyer kept his gaze fastened to the man while he reached to shut her door.

However, reaching was as far as he got.

A shot exploded through the air.

Chapter Fourteen

Sawyer didn't wait to see who'd fired the shot. He shoved Cassidy across the seat and plowed in after her. It wasn't a second too soon because another shot tore through the door where he'd just been standing.

"Is it Willy shooting at us?" Cassidy asked.

Her voice was shaking. The rest of her, too. And he hated that she had to go through something like this again. He'd been a damn fool to take her out of the safe house, and that mistake could end up being a fatal one.

Sawyer cursed himself and lifted his head just slightly so he could look over the dash. He didn't see Willy, but Grayson was in the back of the sheriff's office, where Cassidy had just exited. His gun was drawn, and he was ready to return fire. But like Sawyer, Grayson probably couldn't see the shooter, either.

That, however, didn't stop them from hearing another shot.

"Who's doing this?" Cassidy asked, putting her hands over her ears.

"I'm not sure." But he intended to find out. He stayed in place with his body positioned in front of hers, and he looked around for any signs of the shooter.

Nothing.

To free up his hands, Sawyer shoved the keys in the

ignition, but he didn't turn on the truck's engine. He wanted to be able to hear so he could pinpoint the location of the gunman. Plus, he didn't want to drive away. Not until he knew it was safe. At least here he had backup and not just from Grayson. Mason was inside, too, and with one call, his other cousins could be on the way to help. But if he drove off, trying to get away from the shooter, he might make the situation even more deadly than it already was.

Sawyer's phone buzzed, and he saw Mason's name on the screen. "You see who's doing this?" Sawyer immediately asked him.

"No, but I think the guy's perched on the roof of the building across the street. I thought I saw the sunlight glint on the barrel of a rifle."

"Any chance you can get someone over there to check it out?"

"I'm headed over there now. Gotta clear the streets first though." With that, Mason hung up.

Good thing his cousin had thought of clearing the streets. Sawyer certainly didn't want anyone walking by to be hit with a stray bullet. But just as important he had to keep Cassidy out of the path of any other shots.

Sawyer pinned his gaze to the roof of the building. Took aim.

And waited.

The seconds crawled by. With his heartbeat crashing in his ears. Cassidy's heart was drumming out of control, too, because he could feel her pulse against his back.

Finally, Sawyer saw some movement. Not on the roof where Mason thought the shooter was, but rather on the back corner of the building across the street. It was just a blur of motion, and when Sawyer saw nothing else, he thought maybe it was the sunlight making everything difficult to see.

But no such luck.

The next thing he saw wasn't a blur but someone reaching out from the building. That someone was holding a gun, and he fired a shot right at the truck. The bullet blasted through the window on the passenger's side and sent the safety glass pelting Cassidy and him.

Praying that Mason had indeed gotten the sidewalks cleared, Sawyer levered himself up a little, and using the now-gaping hole in the glass, he returned fire. The gunman ducked out of sight, and before Sawyer could pull the trigger again, another shot came right at them.

This time from the roof.

Hell, there were two of them. At least. And if this was another kidnapping attempt, then the men were taking some huge risks because any one of those bullets could hit Cassidy and kill her.

Another shot came through the glass. The windshield this time. Sawyer shifted his position so he could push Cassidy onto the floor. It wouldn't stop a bullet from reaching her, but it was the best he could do under the circumstances.

Grayson came out the back door and took aim at the roof. Since he had that particular area covered, Sawyer concentrated on the side of the building. He hoped by now that Mason was closing in on these morons.

Sawyer's phone buzzed again, and because he didn't want to look away, he handed it to Cassidy. She hit the answer button, put it on Speaker and almost immediately the sound of a woman's voice poured through the truck.

"Don't shoot," she said.

Even though he had only heard her voice a few times, Sawyer had no trouble recognizing it.

It was Diane.

"Where are you?" Sawyer demanded.

"On the side of a building in Silver Creek. I'm with the man who just fired a shot. But please, don't shoot back because he's using me as a human shield."

Sawyer cursed. That was not what he wanted to hear.

"Listen to her," a man snarled, "or she's right—she'll die."

"Who are you?" Sawyer snapped.

"Somebody who's gonna kill the doc unless you do exactly as I say. We'll trade the doc for Cassidy."

It took Sawyer a moment to get his teeth unclenched. "Not a chance. Why do you want her anyway?"

"This ain't personal," the man said as if that would make everything better. "It's just about the money. We want the other half of that ransom she was supposed to pay for her brother. I figure if we have her, then her brother can pay."

Yeah, but the last time these idiots held a woman captive, she ended up dead. That wasn't going to happen to Cassidy.

"Let Dr. Blackwell go," Sawyer ordered them, though he knew there was no way he could enforce that order. "And then we'll talk."

"I must sound pretty stupid if you think we'd do that," the man snapped. "The doc's not going anywhere until I see Cassidy out of that truck and making her way toward us. You've got three minutes to make up your mind, or we start shootin' again."

"You're not getting Cassidy," Sawyer practically yelled into the phone, but he was talking to the air because the kidnapper had already hung up.

"They won't shoot me," Cassidy said. "I—"

"No." Sawyer had no intention of letting her finish,

because it wasn't even an option on the table. "You're not going out there."

"But they could kill Diane."

"They could kill both of you," Sawyer pointed out. "All of this could be a trick to get you out in the open, and as soon as they get the ransom money, you could end up like April."

Yeah, it was harsh, but she needed to know that he wouldn't budge on this.

"Call Grayson for me," Sawyer instructed.

She did, but Cassidy still didn't stop mumbling about going out there.

"They have Diane," Sawyer said the moment Grayson answered. "She said she's on the side of the building."

Sawyer heard Grayson relay that to his brother. "One of them called Mason," Grayson added to Sawyer a moment later. He paused. "The man told him that they had Bennie, too."

"No!" Cassidy would have bolted from the seat if Sawyer hadn't caught on to her.

"They're probably lying," Sawyer reminded her. "If they had Bennie, don't you think they would have used him instead of Diane?"

That stopped her from struggling, and after a few seconds she gave a shaky nod. "Old habits," Cassidy said under her ragged breath. "It's instinct to try to rescue him."

Sawyer understood that, and he was betting that Bennie's irresponsibility had led Cassidy to rescue him plenty of times. But it wouldn't happen today—even if by some miracle Bennie was indeed out there.

More movement caught his eye, and Sawyer saw Grayson dart out from the back of the sheriff's office, and he hurried across the small parking lot to a building to the right of the vehicles. He had his phone in his left hand and his gun in the other.

"Mason's about a block up from the sheriff's office. He's going to cross the street so he can try to sneak up on the one who's holding Diane," Grayson explained. "We need to distract the shooter on the roof. If he's still there."

And that was a big *if*. It had been minutes since Sawyer had caught a glimpse of the guy, and he could have already come down a fire-escape ladder to join his partner.

"Distract them?" Cassidy asked. "How?"

"With bullets," Sawyer supplied. "It's the only thing that'll get their attention."

Sawyer waited until Grayson took aim and fired. Not at the back of the building, where they had last spotted Diane. Instead, Grayson shot at the front, and Sawyer did the same. The shots were far enough away so they wouldn't ricochet and hit Diane.

He hoped.

"Mason got across," Grayson said a few moments and shots later. "I'm heading over there now." And he took off running up the block so he could approach from the left.

However, Grayson had barely gotten out of sight when Sawyer got more than another glimpse of Diane. Without warning, her captor thrust her out into the open, and this time, he saw that she had her hands cuffed in front of her. She yelled something. A plea that tugged at every lawman's instincts in his body.

Help me.

Sawyer wanted to do just that, but he wouldn't play by the kidnapper's rules.

His phone buzzed again, and Cassidy answered it on speaker.

"How long you want this to go on?" Not one of his cousins. But the kidnapper.

Sawyer opened his mouth to answer "as long as it takes," but he got that prickly feeling going up his spine. The one that told him something other than the obvious wasn't right. Why would the kidnappers want to drag this out when they knew there were lawmen within shooting distance?

They wouldn't draw it out.

They would attack, and if that didn't work, then they'd escape, regroup and make another attempt. Well, this clearly hadn't worked. It was a standoff.

Or was it?

Sawyer whipped around and looked out the back window of the SUV. It wasn't a second too soon. Because he instantly saw an armed man wearing a ski mask. The guy was skulking toward them and was only a few yards from the driver's side of the vehicle. Another second or two and the kidnapper would have been right on them.

"What's wrong?" Cassidy asked.

But Sawyer didn't have time to answer her. He aimed at the man and fired. The bullet hit him squarely in the chest, and despite the fact he was falling to the ground, he pulled the trigger. The shot tore through the SUV. Not just the glass this time. It came through the metal just below the window and slammed into the dash.

Only inches from Cassidy.

And it wasn't the only shot. Others started to pelt the SUV. And they weren't coming from the kidnapper on the ground. Sawyer was pretty sure the guy was dead. These shots came from across the street in front of the sheriff's office. A frantic flurry of gunfire. He couldn't be sure, but he thought the shots weren't just coming from the kidnappers but someone else.

Mason probably.

Sawyer heard a scream, causing his adrenaline to

spike. It hadn't come from Cassidy but from Diane. With her hands still cuffed, he spotted her running away from the building and in the direction Sawyer had last seen Grayson.

Hopefully, Grayson would be able to get the woman out of harm's way. While he was hoping, Sawyer added that Mason would have a clean shot at these morons.

Because Sawyer sure didn't.

He could only sit there, sheltering Cassidy, while the shots continued. He wasn't sure how many seconds passed. It seemed like a million, and with each of those seconds, he realized he could lose Cassidy.

That thought caused him to curse.

Because that shouldn't be on his mind. His entire focus should be on the attack, and that was a clear reminder that his feelings for her had put her in a dangerous situation.

From the corner of his eye, Sawyer spotted Grayson. Alone. And he was taking cover behind one of the vehicles. Obviously, he hadn't been able to get to Diane. He hoped that didn't mean the woman was dead, but it had be a miracle if she managed to get through all of this.

Grayson leaned out of the vehicle, fired a shot at the gunman. From up the street, he could hear Mason do the same. What Sawyer couldn't hear was the gunmen returning fire.

"They're getting away," Sawyer shouted to Grayson.

Sawyer wasn't sure Grayson would be able to hear him over the gunfire, but judging from Grayson's body language, he had. Grayson said something into his phone still clutched in his left hand, and he darted out from cover.

"They can't get away," Cassidy whispered, her voice trembling.

She was right. They needed these criminals behind

bars or the attacks would continue. The next time they might succeed in kidnapping Cassidy. Or killing her.

"Wait with Cassidy," Sawyer shouted to Grayson. "Make sure there aren't others trying to sneak up on us."

Grayson nodded, hurried to the SUV and threw open what was left of the driver's door.

"No. You can't go out there," Cassidy said when Sawyer got out. She tried to hold him by his arm, but he shook off her grip.

"I have to do this." He didn't look down at the fear he knew would be in her eyes.

Sawyer readied his gun and ran toward the kidnappers.

Chapter Fifteen

Cassidy started praying. Sawyer and she had already come close to dying today. His cousins, too. And now Sawyer was perhaps tempting fate again by racing after those gunmen. That only caused her heart to pound even harder, and it slammed against her chest.

Grayson waited with her. He fired glances all around them, no doubt watching to make sure there wasn't another attack. But Cassidy kept her attention on Sawyer.

Until he disappeared from sight.

It sickened her to think of the danger that kept coming at them. Just two days ago, her life had been normal. Sawyer's no doubt had been, too, though his version of normal was far different from hers. He was accustomed to facing situations like this. Well, maybe not the personal attacks. No one should be accustomed to that. But chasing down bad guys was what he did. She prayed he did it today without getting hurt.

"He'll be fine," Grayson said to her.

Cassidy appreciated his attempt to keep her calm, but it wasn't working. Nothing would until this mess was finished. Until the culprits were behind bars and Sawyer was safe.

She braced herself for more gunfire, but none came. Thank goodness. Her thanks went up a significant notch when Sawyer came out of the building. Unharmed. However, she could tell from his expression that he wasn't pleased, and that caused her stomach to drop.

Sawyer made a beeline to the SUV. "The kidnappers aren't back there," he explained. "Neither is Diane. But they have to be nearby. I don't want Cassidy sitting out here waiting, in case they come back for round two."

Grayson nodded. "Take her to the second floor of the sheriff's office. There's an apartment up there, and it's fully wired for security."

Sawyer glanced at the shot-up SUV and his truck. "It'd be stupid to try to drive back to the safe house now," he mumbled, and Sawyer helped her from the SUV. He hurried her toward the back door.

"Stay with her," Grayson called out, heading in right behind them. "I'll get Mason back in here so we can regroup, and I'll send some deputies out to search for Diane and the others."

Sawyer didn't disagree with any of that. They had to find Diane before something horrible happened to her. Cassidy didn't want there to be another April, and with each attack, the chances of someone else dying skyrocketed.

He led her up the stairs just off the back exit. The stairs ended at a short hall that had a single door. When she looked inside, Cassidy saw that the entire second floor made up the apartment. It was one giant open space with a bed on one side, a kitchenette and sitting area straight ahead and a bathroom on the right.

"It used to be the jail before the city built a new one," Sawyer explained. "Some of the deputies crash here when they're pulling extra shifts." He also looked around the room until their gazes met. Then he dragged in a long breath. Shook his head. "I'm sorry."

She reached out, pulled him to her and brushed a kiss on his cheek. "I'm sorry, too."

He flinched. Maybe because it was too dangerous for even a chaste kiss. Not with all this adrenaline and energy inside them. But he also likely objected to her apology itself. In his mind, he should have been able to do something to prevent the latest attack from happening.

"If it hadn't been for you, the kidnappers would have taken me again," she reminded him.

But he didn't seem to believe that, either.

"You should get some rest," he said, tipping his head to the bed and obviously changing the subject. "We'll probably be here awhile."

Cassidy was about to try again to relieve this guilt trip that was weighing him down, but his phone buzzed. Until then, she'd forgotten she was holding it. He'd given it to her during the attack.

Sawyer took it from her and answered it right away. What he didn't do was put the call on speaker. Probably so he could soften any bad news. In other words, he would try to sugarcoat the situation because he would feel she'd already been through enough tonight. So had he, but Sawyer wouldn't see it that way.

Cassidy moved away from him, went to the fridge and took out two bottles of water. Too bad it wasn't hard liquor because she needed something to steady her raw nerves.

So did Sawyer.

She saw the muscles tighten in Sawyer's jaw. But there seemed to be a new hit of adrenaline, too. A new reason for concern. And after he finished the call, she was almost afraid to ask what had caused his reaction. They'd both already had their fill of bad news today, and they didn't need more.

"That was Nate," he started. "While his men were out looking for Diane, he talked with some of her former patients. One of them said Diane had extorted money from him."

Of all the things she'd considered Sawyer might say, that wasn't on the list. This was definitely a new wrinkle in their already too-wrinkled mess.

"Extortion? How?" she asked.

Sawyer wearily shook his head. "According to this former patient, he told Diane of an extramarital affair he was having, and later Diane threatened to tell the man's wife if he didn't pay her ten thousand dollars."

Mercy. If that was true, the charges were serious, and it wouldn't just bring her credibility into question. Diane could lose her license to practice and possibly face some jail time. "Did the man say if he paid Diane?"

"He claims he did. Said he paid her in cash, just as she'd demanded. All of this supposedly went down about a week ago."

So, recently. Probably about the time the kidnappers were putting together their final plans to take Bennie. But that didn't mean the two things were connected.

"Did Nate believe this man?" Cassidy asked.

Sawyer lifted his shoulder. "Yeah, I think he did. But there's a problem. The patient and Diane didn't part on friendly terms, and he's not willing to press charges against her because it would mean telling his wife about the affair. Nate isn't sure if this man is just vindictive, crazy or telling the truth."

Yes, that would be hard to prove. Unless they had bank records. "Didn't you put in a request to get Diane's financials?" Because maybe she'd deposited the ten grand. It wouldn't be absolute proof, but it would be a start if Nate wanted to build a case against Diane.

"Nothing's come back yet. But this latest incident should make it easier to get a court order if necessary."

It might be necessary. In fact, Sawyer might have to conduct a full-scale investigation into Diane's life. Too bad they didn't have time for that because they kept having to dodge bullets. Literally.

"There's more," Sawyer continued a moment later. "You remember hearing that Diane's married, estranged from her very wealthy husband, who's cut her off without a dime?"

"I remember. Willy said she had a drug habit."

He nodded. "Nate hasn't been able to find out the reason for the separation, but there's plenty of gossip about her possible drug use. A criminal informant told Nate that Diane owes a lot of money to her dealer and that she might be desperate to pay the guy off before he exposes her addiction."

It was hard to think of the polished woman she'd seen at the sheriff's office as an addict. But maybe Diane was just very good at hiding her drug use.

And maybe other things, too.

Cassidy had only gotten a glimpse of the woman when she'd run from the kidnappers. She'd certainly looked frightened. But had she been?

Or had it been some kind of ruse?

"Maybe I'm just getting cynical because of the attacks," Cassidy said, "but do you think Diane could be behind the kidnappings and the attempts?"

"I was thinking the same thing," Sawyer readily admitted. "Hard to tell if all of this was an act or not. But the only thing she could have gained from faking her own kidnapping would be to make herself look innocent."

Considering that the kidnappers were looking at a murder charge, maybe Diane believed she had to do something, *anything,* to throw suspicion off herself, and in doing so, had only made it worse.

"It's possible Diane blackmailed April the way she supposedly did this other client," Sawyer added, and he looked at her, hesitating.

And Cassidy knew why.

"Diane could have believed that April would get the money from Bennie," Cassidy finished for him. Before the attacks, she would have dismissed that with the blink of an eye.

She didn't dismiss it now.

And it meant all of this could lead back to Bennie. Diane could have started this by blackmailing April, but Bennie could have finished the botched kidnappings by killing her. However, there was a problem with that theory.

"April wasn't married, so why would Diane have been able to blackmail her about her affair with my brother?" she asked. "And why would Diane think Bennie would have paid to get April back? Yes, an involvement with a woman like April could have maybe hurt his reputation. *Maybe.* But we both know Bennie doesn't have much of a reputation to hurt."

He made a sound of agreement. "Diane could have told April that it would set Willy off to know about the affair."

It would have. Willy had a short fuse when it came to April. And it wouldn't have taken much for Diane to convince Bennie that Willy would come after him. Bennie wasn't a coward, but he wouldn't have wanted a fight with a psycho like Willy.

Still, there was a problem.

"Bennie didn't have the money to pay April's ransom," she reminded him. "He's broke and was trying to get money from me to pay off that bar owner."

"Yeah, but Diane might not have known about that. She probably thought Bennie could just get the money from you."

And in the past, that's exactly what he'd done. This was the first time Cassidy had turned him down, and she wouldn't have done that if she'd known it would lead to all of this.

"But April could have turned the tables on Diane," Sawyer went on. "If April learned that Diane and Bennie were having an affair, she might have tried to press both of them for money to keep the affair quiet."

Yes, because maybe Diane wouldn't have wanted her rich, estranged husband to hear about her affair. Especially with a man of Bennie's character. And that meant they were back to square one. Either April or Diane could have orchestrated the kidnappers. Bennie or Willy, too.

"Bennie," she mumbled, but she obviously didn't say it softly enough. Sawyer heard not just her brother's name but also the emotion that went along with it. And that emotion said loads—that she was worried, and furious, that her brother might be the reason for all this danger.

"I wish there was something I could do to make this go away," he said, the emotion in his voice, too. Then he groaned and scrubbed his hand over his face.

"You've done plenty," she said.

Sawyer's gaze snapped back to hers as if he was looking for any doubts about the truth of that. He wouldn't see doubts because there were none to see. And Cassidy proved that to him by leaning in for a kiss.

She hadn't intended to linger on his mouth, but she did, and soon the lingering turned into so much more.

As it always did with Sawyer.

She felt the need ripple through her body. Maybe

fueled by the fear. Maybe just the basic attraction that had been there all along. Either way, she didn't fight it. Neither did Sawyer, despite the grumble of protest she heard in his throat. Yes, Cassidy knew she should protest it, too.

But she also knew it wouldn't do any good.

She was lost in Sawyer's kiss. In his arms. And she didn't want anyone or anything to snap her back to reality. Here, she could forget all about the danger and the prospect of her brother's guilt. For a few minutes away. She could forget and let Sawyer sweep her away.

It was Sawyer who deepened the kiss. Sawyer who dragged her to him until they were plastered against each other. Body to body so she could feel every inch of him. And there was a lot of him to feel. It didn't take long for her to want more.

Despite the heat rolling through her and making her crazy, she tried to remember where she was. Above the sheriff's office. With Sawyer's lawmen cousins on the floor just below them. Yes, they were no doubt wrapped up in the hunt for Diane and the kidnappers. Wrapped up in the investigation, too. But that didn't mean they wouldn't come by to check on them.

Those thoughts and doubts stayed with her. Until Sawyer's mouth dropped to her neck. She wasn't sure if he remembered that was a hot spot for her or if he'd just gotten lucky. It didn't matter. The kisses robbed her of any doubts and set her body on fire.

Cassidy went after his shirt, but Sawyer didn't exactly cooperate. That's because he was maneuvering her to the door. The wrong direction. She wanted him to take her to the bed.

Without breaking the kiss, he reached around her and

turned the lock. Something she should have thought of. Good thing Sawyer had. She wasn't sure how much privacy they'd actually have, but at least no one could walk in on them.

The kisses continued. Making her crazy. Making her ready to demand a whole lot more, but then Sawyer tore his mouth from hers. And he stared down at her.

Uh-oh.

Cassidy knew what he was going to ask. Did she have any doubts about this? Did she want him to stop?

The answer to both was *no.*

And she let him know that by pulling him back to her. They were already past the point of no return, and if this was going to turn out to be a big mistake, then they might as well make the mistake worth it.

Sawyer made another sound, a rumble deep within his chest, and that seemed to be the green light they needed. He pushed up her top, dropping kisses on her bare stomach before he went to her breasts.

She gasped.

Oh, this was good. Better than she remembered. The kisses caused her legs to feel boneless, and she had no choice but to hold on to Sawyer and let him fire up the heat even hotter. It was wonderful.

But soon, it wasn't enough.

His mouth only made her want more, so while they grappled for kisses, Cassidy got his shirt off and lit some fires of her own. She trailed some kisses down his chest while Sawyer rid her of her clothes.

He was perfect with that toned, lanky cowboy body, she thought as she slid her hands over all those lean muscles. But like the kisses, the touches created their own urgency, and that urgency skyrocketed when her hand slid to the front of his jeans.

"You're playing dirty," he mumbled, and he dragged her back to him so he could take her mouth again.

Sawyer was the one who was playing dirty. She was already well past the foreplay stage, and he still wasn't taking her to bed. Cassidy did something about that. She got them moving in that direction. Not easily. Because with each new frantic wave of kissing, she lost her breath. Maybe her mind, too.

She was wearing just bra and panties as he eased her onto the bed. Finally! The overly soft mattress gave way to their combined weight. "Now," she insisted.

Sawyer was in the process of ridding her of her bra when he looked at her. Not at her breasts. But at her face. And that wasn't a hazed, passionate look he was giving her.

"I don't have a condom," he said.

That didn't cool the fire one bit, but it caused them both to curse, and they began a frenzied search through the nightstand drawer. The relief was instantaneous when she spotted the foil wrappers. She silently thanked his cousins for putting them there.

The urgency soared all over again, and Cassidy and he fought to get rid of the few items of clothing they were still wearing. They fought with the condom, too, and it seemed to take an eternity to get it on.

It had been nearly a year since she'd had Sawyer as a lover, but the memories were still fresh. Still fiery hot. And Cassidy got a fresh reminder of that heat when he slipped inside her. She only had a moment to savor every sensation, and him, before he started to move.

Just like that, she was lost.

In the back of her mind, she knew it shouldn't be this good. This right. Sawyer certainly wasn't hers for the taking, but she had no choice but to let him do just that—take her.

Her body gave way. Surrendering. And Sawyer's face was the last thing she saw before the heat blinded her and sent her over the edge.

Chapter Sixteen

Sawyer felt the release slam through him. In that moment the only thing he could feel was Cassidy. She was the only thing he wanted to feel. And with the taste of her in his mouth and her body trembling beneath his, Sawyer gathered her into his arms and held her close.

Neither of them said a word, but he could practically hear the doubts going through her head. The timing for this sucked. A lot like the last time they'd landed in bed. That time had come on the heels of his investigation into Bennie's wrongdoing.

A lot like now.

Except *now* felt different.

That was probably a bad thing. Every second he spent with her like this only put his mind further away from the investigation. The reminder was enough to get Sawyer moving, but then he looked down at Cassidy. At her bedroom hair. Her eyes.

Yeah, and her body, too.

Hard to miss a beautiful naked woman in his bed. And he suddenly wanted her all over again.

"Don't regret this," she said, her voice all silk and hardly any sound.

He was sure that voice could lure him right back for another round despite the heart-to-heart chat he'd just had with himself. And the lure might have worked just fine if his phone hadn't rung. One glance at the screen, and it was yet another reminder of why he shouldn't lose focus.

"It's your brother," Sawyer let her know, and he tugged on his jeans while he put the phone on the nightstand and hit the speaker button.

"Where's Cassidy?" Bennie immediately asked.

"Safe, with me. Why?" But then Sawyer groaned. "This isn't bad news, is it?"

"You tell me. I just got a call from Willy, and he claims someone tried to kill my sister again while she was with you at the sheriff's office. Any reason I didn't hear about this from Cassidy or you?"

It was a reasonable enough question, but Sawyer didn't care for Bennie's tone. Of course, it could also be because he didn't care for Bennie himself.

"I haven't had time to call you," Cassidy answered. She, too, got up and started dressing. Sawyer got an even better look at her body and felt another punch of heat.

Oh, man.

He was toast when it came to Cassidy.

"Haven't had time?" Bennie repeated. "According to Willy, the attack happened over half an hour ago. You had plenty of time to call me."

"Willy's just chock-full of info today, isn't he?" Sawyer grumbled. "How the heck did he know about the attack anyway?" He already knew the answer, but he wanted to see just how much Bennie knew.

Bennie didn't jump to answer Sawyer's question. Maybe because he knew the reason or maybe because he'd just realized that Willy could have known about the attack because he'd been the one to orchestrate it.

"How did Willy say he'd heard about the shooting?" Sawyer pressed.

"He didn't. And I forgot to ask."

"Convenient," Sawyer mumbled, and he didn't bother trying to sound civil. Cassidy was still partly naked, and he was riled to the core at himself for thinking only about sex at a time like this.

What he should be thinking about was the suspected kidnappers, Bennie and Willy. Willy had been near the sheriff's office just minutes before the shooting, so that would have explained why he'd heard about it. He might have been close enough to hear the bullets flying.

Maybe Willy had even been the one to fire the shots.

But it was interesting that Willy had called Bennie with the news. Maybe he'd done that to stir the proverbial pot. After all, Willy hated Bennie and likely didn't want him to have a peaceful moment in his life. However, it was also interesting that Willy hadn't come into the sheriff's office to tell them anything he might have seen or heard during the attack. Either Willy had something to hide or he didn't want to help them catch the kidnappers.

"Cassidy, what's going on between Sawyer and you?" Bennie came out and asked. "Are you two involved again?"

A muscle flickered in her jaw, and Cassidy paused a moment before she continued to put on her bra. "That's none of your business."

"To hell it's not," Bennie said. "I'm your brother. I care what happens to you, and Sawyer's bad news."

Sawyer had to get his teeth unclenched. "Funny, I feel the same way about you. The difference is—I'm on the right side of the law."

"Yeah, but that doesn't mean you aren't breaking her heart all over again."

A broken heart? This was the first Sawyer was hearing about that. But one look at Cassidy's face, and he thought there might be something to it. Bennie had definitely hit a nerve, but still that didn't mean he would discuss it with her brother.

"Is there a point to this call?" Cassidy asked Bennie at the same moment she dodged Sawyer's gaze.

"No point. Just a warning. You know what you went through last time—"

However, Bennie didn't get a chance to finish. Cassidy reached over and hit the end call button. She continued to dress, with her back to him. And she didn't say a word. So, Sawyer went to her, took her by the arm and turned her around.

"Is he right?" Sawyer asked, but he left off that broken-heart detail that Bennie had mentioned. If it was true, then maybe Cassidy would be the one to spell it out.

She opened her mouth. Closed it. Looked away again. "Does it matter?"

"Yeah." But Sawyer wasn't sure he wanted to hear the answer.

They'd parted ways in a fit of anger, but he'd figured that Cassidy hadn't given him another thought. Certainly, she hadn't had a broken heart.

Had she?

"Drop the subject," she insisted.

Mercy, the sex must have turned his brain to mush because he didn't want to do that even if this was a conversation he was pretty sure he should avoid. However, Sawyer didn't get a chance to press her. His phone rang again, and he snatched it up, prepared to tell Bennie to take a hike. But it wasn't Bennie.

It was Grayson.

"I just got a call from the tech at the lab," Grayson greeted. "About a half hour ago, someone stole Bennie's DNA sample."

A theft at the lab? Well, there was only one person who'd want to do that.

Bennie himself.

No one else would care if Bennie's DNA proved that he was Emma's father.

"The lab has surveillance," Grayson continued, "and they're emailing me the footage now. Thought you'd like to see the thief."

"I would," Sawyer said reaching for the rest of his clothes. "I'll be right down."

CASSIDY HAD TO HURRY to keep up with Sawyer as he barreled down the stairs from the apartment. She totally understood the reason for rushing. The person on the surveillance footage was likely the person behind the attacks. But Cassidy wished she'd had a little more time to come to terms with it.

Especially since it might be Bennie's face they were about to see.

She rethought that and took out the *might*. It was *likely* that Bennie had stolen his DNA sample, and the most obvious reason for doing that was because he suspected he was Emma's father. And if he was and was trying to hide it, then Bennie himself might have been the one who set up the kidnappings.

That stalled the air in her lungs.

If Bennie had been the one to try to kill her, then he'd partly succeeded. Something like that would crush her heart. And where would it leave baby Emma? With a dead mother and perhaps a father who'd commit murder so that no one would know he was her father.

"Are you okay?" Sawyer asked, glancing at her over his shoulder.

Because his gaze dropped to her mouth, Cassidy

touched her fingers to her lips. It was an instant reminder of the kisses that had led to them falling into bed. And she hoped Sawyer's cousins couldn't see the telltale signs of how she felt. She had enough to deal with without their questioning glances.

"I'm fine," she mumbled.

Even though it was an obvious lie, it was enough to get him moving again to Grayson's office, where the sheriff and his brother Mason were peering at a computer screen.

"Nothing yet," Grayson immediately let them know. "It's not actual footage but rather pictures taken at three-second intervals." He paused, looked at Sawyer. "We've learned it wasn't just Bennie's sample that was taken. The baby's was, too. And so were your DNA results that Quantico sent over for comparison."

Sawyer pulled back his shoulders. "Why the heck would someone steal mine?"

Grayson shrugged. "Maybe to make you look guilty."

He was right, but Cassidy knew that Sawyer hadn't been involved in the theft because he'd been with her nonstop for the past two days. Besides, he wouldn't do anything like that. If Emma was his, he'd want to know. He darn sure wouldn't be trying to hide it.

"We have to go through the surveillance frame by frame," Mason added in a grumble. He checked his watch, mumbled something else that she didn't catch.

They stood there, watching, waiting, as the photos scrolled past on the screen. "Where are the others?" Sawyer asked, tipping his head to the deputies' offices that lined the hall.

"Dade's up front, working the desk and making sure no one gets inside here. Bree's out with the Texas Rangers, looking for Diane and those gunmen. I also sent

Gage to the safe house. I figured after the attack here, it wouldn't hurt to have the extra security."

"Thank you," Cassidy and Sawyer said in unison. With everything going on, she certainly hadn't forgotten about Emma's safety, and she was glad Grayson was doing everything to make sure those gunmen didn't find the safe house.

Or return to the sheriff's office for another attack.

"Bennie called right before we came downstairs," Sawyer said. "He claimed Willy told him about the shooting. Any chance Willy was still nearby when those shots were flying?"

"It's possible. And it's possible he knew about the shooting because he's the one who hired those men. I haven't ruled him out as a suspect."

Cassidy held on to that hope. Because it would mean Bennie was innocent. Plus, Willy did indeed have motive if he'd wanted to collect that steep ransom and get revenge on Bennie and April for their affair. Willy could do that all at once by setting Bennie's kidnapping in motion.

But even Willy couldn't have anticipated the problems.

And there were definitely problems because the attacks had continued. Cassidy was so tired of Emma and everyone being in danger that she considered trying to negotiate with Willy.

Briefly considered it, anyway.

She could offer him the rest of the ransom to back off, but if it turned out Willy was innocent, then she wouldn't have the money to pay off the real kidnappers if they managed to take Emma or her. She prayed it didn't come down to that, but not many things had gone her way.

A phone rang, and Mason jumped. He scrambled to take the cell from his jeans' pocket and nearly dropped it when he managed to retrieve it.

"Yeah?" he answered.

Grayson stopped everything and watched his brother. The conversation didn't last long, and Mason headed for the door, nearly plowing into them.

"Abbie's in labor," Mason called back to them. And a split second later, he disappeared out the back exit.

Despite everything else going on, Grayson smiled. So did Sawyer.

"We've never thought of Mason as the fatherly type," Sawyer explained to Cassidy. Then he lifted his shoulder. "Like me. People always said Mason and I were a lot alike."

Maybe it was her imagination, but there seemed to be a warning in the mix. Maybe he was telling her that sex hadn't changed things between them.

And it hadn't.

Okay, it had.

It had changed things for her anyway. It had only deepened her feelings for him. But she couldn't let Sawyer know that. The last thing she wanted was to pressure him into a relationship that he obviously didn't want. Maybe because he still didn't fully trust her. Or maybe because he truly wasn't the relationship/father type.

Cassidy was in such deep thought about that, and it took her a moment to realize the air had changed in the room. That's because something on the screen had caught Sawyer's and Grayson's attention. Except it wasn't something.

It was *someone*.

The lab door opened and a person dressed in dark clothes stepped inside.

"Why didn't a security alarm go off?" Sawyer immediately asked.

"Someone disabled it," Grayson answered, obviously

not pleased about that. "We're lucky it was discovered so soon. The lab supervisor realized he'd forgotten something at work, and he went back in to get it. That's when he noticed that someone had tampered with the security system and stolen the DNA samples. He did a quick check of the security feed and figured out it had happened about a half hour earlier."

Sawyer mumbled some profanity. "It's an inside job then. Someone was paid off to make this happen."

"Yeah," Grayson verified. "The supervisor's questioning everyone now. Someone might confess, and if they don't, he might be able to use their badges to determine where everyone was. All the employees have badges, and the system registers their comings and goings."

That meant they might find out who'd orchestrated this break-in at the lab. Of course, they might learn that themselves if they could see the intruder's face.

So far, that hadn't happened.

The person kept his head down as if he knew the placement of the camera. Probably did since an employee could have given them that information, as well.

Cassidy held her breath when the intruder moved closer to the camera and toward what appeared to be a storage locker. Still no view of the person's face, and because he was wearing a bulky black coat, she couldn't even get a sense of his size.

But it could be Bennie.

She wasn't sure which would be worse—not seeing the face at all or seeing it and knowing it was her brother who was trying to obstruct justice.

"There," Grayson said, and he froze the screen. Finally, they had a partial view of the face, but it was grainy, and the angle didn't help.

With some clicks on the laptop, Grayson zoomed

in. It still wasn't enough, so he went to the next shot and zoomed in again. Little by little, the image became clearer.

And this time, Cassidy could see the intruder's face.

She'd braced herself for what she might see there, but she obviously hadn't braced herself enough.

Oh, God.

Chapter Seventeen

"Diane," Sawyer spat out like profanity. "She keeps turning up like a bad penny."

He didn't have to ask what the heck she was doing there because he could see her taking the DNA samples from the storage vault. She also did something on the computer—probably deleting his DNA info that Quantico had sent over.

"Why would she steal the samples and destroy Sawyer's info?" Cassidy asked, taking the question right out of his mouth.

Sawyer hoped the answer to that was in the security photos themselves because they had no idea where Diane was now. Last he'd seen her, she had been with the kidnappers.

Yet here she was.

Or at least she had been at the lab about forty-five minutes earlier.

"She doesn't look injured," Cassidy said, obviously remembering the blood they'd found on the warehouse floor where she'd supposedly been kidnapped. There hadn't been enough blood to indicate a serious injury, but the blood had to come from somewhere. Or rather, someone. That bulky coat she was wearing could conceal plenty of things.

Grayson clicked to the next photo, and it showed Diane slipping the two samples into her pocket. The next was a clearer shot of her face, and she was looking over her shoulder at the door.

"Someone's there," Grayson pointed out at the exact moment that Sawyer saw it, too. The shadowy figure standing in the door.

Grayson tried to zoom in on it, but the person was too far away, and it only made the shot blurrier. Parts of it anyway. The one part that was crystal clear was the person's hand.

And the gun he was holding.

"Diane's kidnapper could have forced her to steal the samples," Sawyer concluded with a huff. "Or she armed him and placed him in the doorway to make herself look innocent."

There was nothing in Diane's body language to clue them in. Yes, the woman looked nervous, but she likely would whether she was innocent or guilty. After all, she was breaking into a lab and stealing evidence from a murder investigation.

And that meant they were back to square one.

Well, unless they could get something from the supervisor to prove which of his techs had helped with this crime. But that would take time.

"I'll have one of the FBI-lab guys drive over from San Antonio," Sawyer said, taking out his phone. "This time, the supervisor will run the tests here. With me standing over his shoulder."

He called the FBI tech first, and when he got verification that someone was on the way, Sawyer phoned Gage, who was at the safe house, to let him know they needed another sample of Emma's DNA.

"You want me to bring her there?" Gage asked.

"No. Stay put. I'll come out there and collect it myself." That way, Emma would stay safe. The last place he wanted her was in Silver Creek, where the most recent attack had occurred. "How is she?"

"Sleeping like a baby. In other words, she's waking up a lot."

Sawyer figured that was normal, but he hated to think that Emma might be picking up on the stress of everyone around her. And that was an awful lot of stress for one so young.

He ended the call with Gage so he could make another one. Thankfully, Sawyer didn't have to hunt for the number because it was in the recent calls on his phone.

"You're bringing in Bennie?" Cassidy asked.

Sawyer nodded, pressed the number, but it went straight to voice mail. He left Bennie a message ordering him to the Silver Creek sheriff's office ASAP.

"If Bennie arrives before I get back from the safe house," Sawyer told Grayson, "get the DNA sample and hold him."

Grayson nodded. "I'll have Dade cover the office so I can go with you." He paused, looked at Sawyer. "Unless you'd rather I stay here with Cassidy."

"No," Cassidy said without hesitation. "I want to go with Sawyer. Besides, the gunmen attacked us here. It might not be safe for us to stay."

Sawyer couldn't argue with that, and besides, he didn't like the idea of Cassidy and him being apart as long as the danger was out there. And he hoped like the devil that his feelings didn't have anything to do with what had happened in the bed upstairs. He had to think with his head. That was the best way to keep Cassidy and Emma safe.

Sawyer retrieved a DNA swab packet from the supply closet while Grayson went to the front of the building to talk to his brother. When Grayson returned, he handed Sawyer a set of keys. "It's for Dade's truck, which is parked out front. He's kept his eyes on it to make sure no one slips on a tracking device."

Good idea. He couldn't risk leading the kidnappers straight to the baby. This trip would be risky enough as it was.

They headed to the door, but when they reached it, Sawyer drew his gun and moved in front of Cassidy. So did Dade and Grayson.

Sawyer didn't see anyone or anything suspicious, but he knew from experience that someone could be there. He hurried to the truck and drove it onto the sidewalk, close to the door. So close that Cassidy had only a few seconds outside before she climbed into the cab of the truck. Grayson followed her inside, and Sawyer sped away.

"We'll have to drive around for a while," Sawyer let her know. "To make sure we aren't being followed."

She nodded. Didn't say a word. But because her arm was pressed against his, he felt the muscles tense. Sawyer wished he could say something to take the edge off the tension, but it was hard to reassure her that all would be well when both he and Grayson kept their guns in hand.

Keeping watch all around them, Sawyer drove out of town. It was barely dark, and the vehicles both behind and ahead of them had on their lights, making it easier for him to see if there was a possible threat. But one by one, the cars turned, and the lights from town faded when he reached the farm road.

There wasn't much of a moon, but he turned on the high beams so he could see the sides of the road. There wasn't much of a shoulder, either, but it was still wide enough for someone to have parked to wait for them.

Sawyer turned on to another road and watched for

anyone trying to follow them. But again, there was no one. After several more turns, he decided it was time to head to the safe house. He made a quick turn on to a farm road so he could backtrack.

But he immediately spotted a problem.

Ahead of them were some cows, all milling around right in the middle of the road, and Sawyer had no choice but to slam on his brakes. The sound of the tires squealing on the asphalt got them moving. So did a few taps of the horn. That's when he realized how big of a herd it was.

At least a hundred.

Some ambled behind the truck to get away from the sound of the horn. He couldn't risk hitting them. A collision at such slow speed wouldn't kill the cows, but it could disable the engine and strand Cassidy and him.

"Did someone do this?" Cassidy asked.

Sawyer was about to point out the remnants of the white-woods fence to their left and tell her that cattle often broke fence. After all, they were on the perimeter of a large ranch where something like that could easily happen. But he stopped when he saw movement just off the road.

Not cows.

But a person.

And Sawyer couldn't be sure, but it looked as if someone had a gun pointed right at them.

CASSIDY SAW THE BLUR of motion for just a split second, but a blur was all that she managed.

"Get down!" Sawyer and Grayson said in unison, and it was Sawyer who pushed her down on the seat. It was a tight fit between the two men, and they both leaned over, protecting her.

But from what?

"What did you see?" she asked and wasn't sure she wanted to know the answer.

It was several long moments before Sawyer said anything. "Maybe just a hunter." He paused. "Maybe a gunman."

Her heart went to her throat, and the terror shot through her. Not fear for herself but for Sawyer and his cousin.

For Emma, too.

"How far are we from the safe house?" Cassidy blurted out.

"Far enough," Sawyer assured her. "A good ten miles or more." He kept his attention pinned to their surroundings, and like Grayson, kept a dead grip on his weapon. "I wasn't even headed in the right direction."

That was something at least. She couldn't bear the thought of Emma being in danger again. But if the kidnappers had found them, then maybe they'd found Emma, too. She needed to call Gage to make sure everything was okay. However, she reached for Sawyer's phone just as he threw the truck into Reverse, only to immediately slam on the brakes. The jolt knocked her hand away.

She glanced behind them, following Sawyer's gaze when she heard him curse. It took Cassidy a moment to realize why he'd done that. She saw the cattle behind them. In front of them, too. If there was truly a gunman out there, then they couldn't move unless it would be to the left, where there were the remnants of a broken white wooden fence.

"You see him?" Grayson asked.

But Sawyer shook his head. "He must have moved."

Not exactly a comforting thought since he could be using the cattle for cover closing in for a better shot.

But there was something about that theory that didn't make sense.

"How would the kidnappers even know we were out here?" Cassidy asked.

Sawyer shook his head. "Good question. But I don't know the answer."

Well, they hadn't been followed, and since Dade had kept watch on his truck, there wasn't a good chance that someone had planted a tracking device on it.

But there was a slim chance.

That certainly didn't steady her fears or her heartbeat. Willy had been at the sheriff's office. Diane had been spotted near there, too. Maybe one of them had managed to get to Dade's truck or any of the other vehicles they would have used. After all, the suspects knew that Sawyer and she were at the sheriff's office, and it wouldn't have been a stretch for them to assume they'd be leaving soon.

And headed back to the safe house.

"I need to call Gage," she said on a rise of breath.

Sawyer didn't question why, and she could see the concern on his face, too. He handed her the phone but kept his attention on their surroundings.

Thankfully, Gage's number wasn't hard to find, and he answered on the first ring. "Trouble?" he asked before she could say a word.

"Maybe. Someone might have followed us." She had to swallow hard before she could continue. "There might be a gunman. Is Emma okay?" And she held her breath, waiting and praying.

"Yeah. She's fine, but I'll head to the front window and keep watch. If anyone comes down that road, I'll know it."

Cassidy reminded herself that Gage was a capable

lawman, and between him and the other deputy, it would be enough to keep Emma safe. "Thanks."

"You need me to call backup?" Gage asked.

She looked up at Sawyer to repeat the question, but he just shook his head. "I want everyone to stay put until we know what we're dealing with. This might be a trick to draw Gage away from the safe house."

If so, it wouldn't work. No way would Cassidy put Sawyer's or her safety ahead of the baby's.

"Keep me posted," Gage said, and she ended the call.

Sawyer honked his horn again to try to budge the cows, and he must have seen an opening because he started to back up. Not speeding but rather creeping along while Grayson fastened his attention to the front of the vehicle.

It seemed to take an eternity for them to go a few inches, and because she was watching Sawyer so closely, she saw the change in his expression. Relief, maybe? He pushed his foot harder on the accelerator, taking them away from the herd and the possible gunman.

However, the relief was very short-lived.

"Look out!" Grayson shouted.

His warning barely had time to register in Cassidy's mind, when there was a swishing sound. It took her a moment to realize that it wasn't the wind or a cow brushing against the truck.

Someone had fired a shot through a silencer.

The bullet tore through the windshield and flung the safety glass right at them.

Sawyer hit the accelerator again, only to have to brake because of the cows. "I can't see behind us," he let Grayson know. "Where's the shooter?"

"Just ahead to the right. I only got a glimpse of him," Grayson said, lowering his window.

Another shot came at them. Also fired from a gun rigged with a silence. Then, another shot. But this time it didn't just come from the front of the truck.

It came from behind them.

More glass crashed onto them, this time from the rear window. So, not just one gunman. But two. At least.

"They're shooting high," Sawyer mumbled.

Cassidy's mind was whirling with all sorts of bad thoughts, and it took her a moment to realize the high shots probably meant the shooters weren't trying to kill them. This was probably another kidnapping attempt. But it didn't matter. Any one of those shots could still hit them.

"There's a truck behind us blocking the road," Sawyer warned them.

No. This couldn't be happening. They couldn't drive forward because of the cattle and the shooter. But now there was at least one shooter behind them, too.

They were trapped.

Chapter Eighteen

Hell. Sawyer knew he had to get them out of there, but he didn't have a lot of options. The cows were still ahead, and he couldn't go in reverse, either, because of the vehicle behind them.

His only option was the left side.

There were only a few cattle there and beyond them, a pasture. The truck could easily break through what was left of the white wooden fence, but first he'd have to get past the ditch.

More bullets slammed into the roof of the truck. A stark reminder that he didn't have to time to debate his decision.

"Hold on," Sawyer warned them.

He turned the steering wheel to the left and hit the accelerator. Maybe, just maybe, the ditch wouldn't be too deep and he could clear it. And while he was hoping, he added that none of those shots would stray into the cab of the truck. So far, they'd been lucky, but he hated that Cassidy's life hinged on luck.

The truck lurched forward toward the fence and came to a dead stop when the front tires hit the ditch. The jolt was as bad as if he'd had a collision, and it slung them all forward. If they hadn't been wearing their seat belts, the impact would have sent them flying through the windshield.

"What happened?" Cassidy asked.

He hated to tell her, but she had to know. "We didn't clear the ditch." The cattle had obviously made it worse by trudging through it, and the truck's tires had instantly bogged down in the mud and the muck.

The shots continued—all muffled with a silencer maybe so that the sound wouldn't spook the cows. Again, all the shots were high, tearing through the roof of the truck. And worse, Sawyer could tell the shooters were moving closer. Ready to do whatever they'd come here to do. His guess was they would kidnap Cassidy.

Or they'd try.

He wouldn't stand by and let her be taken. But Grayson and he were almost certainly expendable. Unless the kidnappers planned to hold them all for ransom. Either way, a lot could go wrong in the next couple of minutes.

Because he had no choice, he texted Gage and asked for backup. Not from Gage himself. Sawyer wanted his cousin and the ranch hands with the baby, but Gage could ask for help from the sheriff of a nearby town. Of course, that kind of backup would take a long time to get there.

The bullets had already torn away most of the front windshield. Sawyer used the butt on his gun to knock down the rest. "Climb through, and we'll use the front of the truck for cover."

He hoped. But at least if they were outside, he'd be able to better see the location of their attackers.

"I'll cover my side," Grayson said to him. "You cover yours."

"Stay down," Sawyer added, and he rid Cassidy and himself of their seat belts.

He helped Cassidy maneuver through the gaping hole

and onto the hood of the truck. It was hot from the engine and littered with glass. The flying bullets sure didn't help. Still, he got her to the front of the truck and positioned himself so that she was sandwiched between Grayson and him.

"They want to kidnap me," Cassidy said. "I need to get in front of both of you. They won't shoot me."

"Not going to happen," Sawyer quickly let her know. But he wasn't exactly sure how he would get them out of this mess. He only knew he had no choice but to succeed.

Another shot rang out. And this one wasn't silenced. The sound blasted through the night.

"Watch out!" Grayson practically shouted.

Since Sawyer had his attention on the direction of the shooter, he didn't see what was coming at them from behind.

More cattle.

And these weren't loping around.

They were running right toward them, and it meant they were in the middle of a stampede. The cows couldn't run through the truck, but in a panic, they could trample all of them.

Sawyer caught onto Cassidy and moved her back onto the hood of the truck. As before, he and Grayson tried to position themselves to best protect her. But the shots just kept coming. And this time they weren't hitting the roof of the truck.

They were coming right at them.

"Get Cassidy back in the truck," Grayson insisted. "I'll try to stop these guys."

He didn't give Sawyer a chance to disagree—something he definitely would have done. Grayson was a husband and father, and despite that sheriff's badge clipped to his belt, Sawyer didn't want him taking these risks.

This was his fight, and he should be the one going after the gunmen.

Grayson eased off the hood, and staying close to the truck, he worked his way to the back.

"Let's go," Sawyer told Cassidy, and he started the trek over the hood and back into the cab. They moved fast. Had to. The bullets were coming at them nonstop now.

"If you want her to live, you'll let her go," someone shouted. Sawyer didn't recognize the voice.

The truck's headlights were still on, and it was enough for Sawyer to see the frozen look on Cassidy's face. "It might be the only way to get us out of this," she whispered. "They won't kill me. They only want the ransom money."

That argument wasn't going to work, and he pushed her down onto the floor of the truck. "Remember what they did to April. They probably hadn't planned to kill her, either."

Well, unless April had double-crossed them in some way. And there was the problem—Sawyer didn't know who was behind the bullets, and it might not even matter. Cassidy could end up like April if these goons got their hands on her.

"At least consider it," Cassidy said.

He paused a heartbeat. "Considered it, and the answer's no. You're not sacrificing yourself for me or anyone else."

And he hoped that put an end to any further argument because he wanted to focus on their attackers and not talk about something that wasn't going to happen—ever.

The shots slowed until there were several seconds between each one. Sawyer hoped that didn't mean the gunmen were closing in on them. Instead, maybe it meant they were low on ammo, but he didn't think he, Cassidy and his cousin would be that lucky.

He could no longer see Grayson. His cousin had disappeared amid the cattle and the darkness. Grayson was a smart lawman, and maybe he'd be able to stop at least one of the shooters. That would leave the other for Sawyer. Maybe there were just two of them, and he could manage to get Cassidy safely away from here. If he did, he was moving her straight to the safe house, where she would stay until he had arrested every person involved in this mess.

And he *would* arrest them.

No way would he let them get away with this.

Sawyer heard the shot on the left side of the truck. Maybe it had come from Grayson because the angle and sound were different from the others. He waited, listening, but there were no other shots and nothing from Grayson to indicate what had just happened.

Some movement from the corner of his eye caught his attention, and Sawyer looked into what was left of the side mirror. The broken pieces created an eerie broken image of the moving cows. No gunmen though.

But Sawyer quickly amended that.

There was someone using the cattle for cover.

"Stay down," he said to Cassidy, and Sawyer adjusted his position so he could blast this idiot to smithereens.

He fastened his attention to the spot where he'd last seen the person, and it didn't take him long to get another glimpse. And then a look at the face.

Hell.

EVEN THOUGH SAWYER didn't say a word, Cassidy could tell from his body language that something else had just gone wrong. She prayed something bad hadn't happened to Grayson or that they weren't about to be ambushed.

She lifted her head just enough to follow Sawyer's gaze, and her shoulders snapped back. *No.* It couldn't be. But it was. She could see the person staring straight at them.

Bennie.

Oh, God. He'd been the one behind this.

Her chest tightened into a vise. Her breath vanished. It felt as if someone had taken hold of her heart and was crushing the life right out of it.

"I'm sorry," Sawyer said a split second before he shoved her back down. Out of the line of possible fire. Sawyer's gaze also fired all around them, probably looking for the second gunman.

But Cassidy couldn't stay down. She couldn't let her brother finish what he'd obviously started, and she couldn't sit by while he shot Grayson or Sawyer.

"Bennie, don't do this!" Cassidy called out.

She wasn't sure what kind of reaction she'd get, but Cassidy was a little surprised when Bennie just stood there and shook his head.

"Sawyer, don't shoot," Bennie added, surprising her even more.

Sawyer must not have anticipated that response either because he mumbled, "What the heck's going on?"

Cassidy had no idea.

However, that didn't stop Sawyer from taking aim at Bennie. "Put down your gun and get your hands in the air so I can see them," Sawyer ordered, sounding very much like the lawman that he was.

But Bennie shook his head. "I can't. I'm not armed. And my hands are tied."

Sawyer glanced at her to see if she knew what this was all about, but she had to shake her head, too.

"Don't you get it?" Bennie snapped. "Someone kidnapped me again. That's why I'm out here. The kidnapper brought me to you."

"It might be a trick," Sawyer whispered.

Cassidy was already considering it. Her brother could be so desperate for money that he'd be willing to fake his kidnapping twice. And in doing so, he could have put them all in danger—again.

"Who kidnapped you?" Cassidy pressed.

He didn't jump to answer that. In fact, he seemed to dodge her gaze. Never a good sign. "The same men who kidnapped you and me before," he finally said. "They grabbed me and put me in the truck." He tipped his head to the vehicle on the road. "They used a tracker to follow you."

"A tracker?" she repeated, and Cassidy certainly didn't make it sound as if she believed him. Because she didn't. "Did you put some kind of tracking device on the truck?"

"Not me," Bennie insisted. He shook his head, repeated it. "But someone did. One of the men, I suspect. When I saw what they were doing, I tried to warn you, but I couldn't get to one of their phones."

She hoped that was true, that her brother had tried to help her, but again, Cassidy wasn't sure. What they needed were answers.

"You must know who brought you here," Sawyer challenged. "And how the heck did the kidnappers get past the cop guarding you?"

Bennie opened his mouth to speak, but he didn't get a chance to say anything else. A guy wearing a dark ski mask came up behind him, and Cassidy had no trouble seeing the gun that he jammed against Bennie's head. She also had no trouble seeing her brother's reaction.

He was terrified.

Cassidy's own reaction was automatic. There was that overwhelming need to protect him. She'd done it for so long that it had become second nature. But she couldn't let her second nature get Sawyer and Grayson killed. Because Bennie could have hired the man with the gun to convince her that he'd indeed been kidnapped. If so, it was very convincing. That gun was real, and the man's finger was on the trigger.

"Cassidy, you've got one choice and one choice only," the man threatened. "Surrender or your brother dies where he stands. I figure you got less than ten minutes to make up your mind about it because that's when the boss gets here."

That thinned her breath, and her pulse was crashing in her ears, making it hard for her to hear. She forced herself to remember that the threat could be another part of the setup to draw her out into the open. Not that Sawyer would have let her anyway, but Cassidy had no plans to surrender.

Well, unless it was the only way she could save Sawyer.

Something he definitely wouldn't appreciate.

There was no chance she could convince Sawyer that this was her fault. She should have seen what Bennie was up to and nixed it. She should have stopped him before anyone got hurt. And that was something she'd have to learn to live with. Still, that didn't make the pain in her heart any easier.

"Who's your boss?" Sawyer snapped.

"Wouldn't you like to know," the gunman taunted. "Guess you'll find out soon enough, won't you?"

Judging from the profanity Sawyer mumbled, that

didn't help him choke back the anger. Cassidy was having a hard time choking it back, too, but it wasn't the only emotion she was feeling.

"Bennie, why is this happening?" she asked. Her voice broke. She thought she might break, too. This was tearing her heart into a dozen little pieces, and she doubted it would get better any time soon. "Just how deep are you mixed up in this?"

Her brother didn't jump to deny his innocence. He only shook his head and looked away again as if he was afraid she'd see the guilt in his eyes. But Cassidy could see it without eye contact. Everything about Bennie's body language told her what she didn't want to hear.

"How deep?" she pressed, her voice raised.

Bennie groaned softly but still didn't look at her. "I didn't mean for it to come to this. I swear, I didn't."

That was it—his admission of guilt. Something she'd prayed she wouldn't hear and yet something Cassidy had already expected.

"You did it for the money," she said. And it wasn't a question. Only money drove Bennie, and this time there was a lot of money at stake. "You needed to pay off that bar owner."

He nodded. Groaned again. "He would have killed me. Maybe killed you, too. I thought I was saving us both."

"You thought you were saving yourself," Cassidy argued.

"I was thinking of you, too!" Bennie shouted back.

"Enough of this," Sawyer snarled. He gave her a look. One of sympathy. But it didn't last long. His jaw muscles turned to iron when he looked at Bennie. "Tell your henchman to put down his gun," he added.

"He's not my henchman," Bennie insisted.

"Right," Sawyer said. "You hired him. Now, tell him to drop the weapon or you both die."

Cassidy didn't think that was a bluff. Bennie had obviously gone too far over the edge to be saved. All it would take was for the gunman to make a move to shoot again, and Sawyer would have no choice but to fire first. With Bennie between them, he could easily be shot.

"I hired him," Bennie admitted, his voice low and weary. "But he no longer works for me. I pulled out of the kidnapping plan. Or rather, I tried to do that, but they wouldn't let me get out."

Cassidy stared at him. "What do you mean?"

"I needed that money. You knew that. I told you I needed it—"

"You never said you'd be killed because of it," she interrupted, "or that you'd be willing to risk my life to get it."

"Your life was already at risk. The loan shark who owns the bar would have come after you if I hadn't done something. I was desperate to save us both."

"Stop all this yakking," the gunman growled. "I thought I was pretty clear when I said what had to happen. I'll trade Bennie for his sister, and that's gotta happen before the boss gets here. After that, all bets are off, and I start shooting."

"You were clear, all right," Sawyer agreed, "but if you think I'll turn Cassidy over to you or your boss, think again. You need to come up with a different plan. One that involves putting your gun on the ground and surrendering."

Grayson was out there, somewhere, and hopefully could step up to help. Maybe the backup would be here soon, too.

The gunman laughed. "Hey, it's not my plan. I'm just

following orders. And if you think I won't ice ol' Bennie here, then think again. He's not playing on our team anymore. But I tell you, when he was playing for us, he was real eager to put that kidnapping plan into action. Desperate men sure do stupid, desperate things."

Cassidy had to get her teeth unclenched. Bennie had been desperate, all right, but it had been of his own making. No one had forced him to get involved with a loan shark.

"So, you faked our kidnapping so I'd pay up and never know the truth about what you'd done." Again, Cassidy wasn't asking a question. She was pretty sure where this was going, and it wasn't a direction she liked.

"I changed my mind," Bennie argued. "I tried to call it off, but these goons said they'd kill April if I didn't go through with it."

"April?" Sawyer and she questioned in unison.

It wasn't much of a surprise that the woman's name had come up. April had clearly been involved in some kind of way with the kidnapping. But until now Cassidy hadn't known if April was a victim or the person behind the abductions.

She knew it now.

"Why would they threaten to kill April?" Sawyer asked.

Despite having a gun pressed against his head, Bennie took his time answering. "Because they thought they could use her to make sure that I cooperated."

"Tell 'em," the gunman snarled when Bennie paused. "They'll get a kick out of hearing this."

But Bennie still didn't belt out an explanation for several long moments. "The baby's mine," he finally said. "April had a test. An amnio, and it proved I was the father. These goons said they'd use the baby and her to make sure I collected the ransom money."

Cassidy touched her fingers to her lips. It was so hard to hear this. Hard to learn that Bennie was Emma's father and that these monsters wanted to use the newborn as a pawn.

"Emma's yours," Sawyer said under his breath. Not loud.

But plenty loud enough for Cassidy to hear him and the emotion in his voice. He had to be feeling so many things right now, but he was no doubt pushing them aside because of that gunman.

Cassidy tried to do the same—push the emotion aside. Hard to do. Here, all this time, she'd been with her own blood kin, her niece, at that, and she hadn't even known it.

"You killed April?" Sawyer asked her brother.

"No." Bennie not only shouted his answer, he frantically shook his head. "It was one of them." He tipped his head to the man behind him.

"Yeah, it was me," the man readily answered. He checked his watch. "Now, time's up for Bennie here. Either come and trade places with him or he dies."

The demand didn't make sense because the gunman could ask for ransom from her for Bennie's release. So, there had to be more.

But what?

And just how many more crimes would her brother confess to before the night was over? Maybe a confession to the ultimate one—that *he* was the boss.

"What are you not telling me?" Cassidy demanded, and she aimed a glare right at Bennie.

But he didn't answer.

Because the shot cracked through the air. Not fired from the gun near her brother. This had come from the

other side of the truck where she'd last seen Grayson.
Cassidy couldn't see him now, but the cows that were
still nearby started to run again.

Something or someone had stampeded them.

As if in a panic, some of the cows bashed into the side
of the truck. And the panic wasn't just on that side but
where Bennie was standing, as well. The masked man
with the gun cursed, hooked his arm around Bennie's
neck and yanked him back.

That's when Cassidy saw that her brother's hands were
indeed tied.

And she saw something else.

Another person dressed all in black walking through
the cows and directly toward them.

That person took aim at Sawyer and fired.

Chapter Nineteen

Sawyer pulled Cassidy down onto the seat but not before he got a good look at the person who'd just shot at them.

Diane.

She certainly didn't look like a woman who'd recently been kidnapped. Just the opposite. Unlike Bennie, her hands weren't tied and no one was holding a gun to her head. Sawyer didn't know exactly how Diane fit into all of this, but he intended to find out.

He glanced in Bennie's direction to make sure the gunman there wasn't about to start firing, as well. But the goon didn't look on the verge of pulling the trigger. He had his hands full with Bennie struggling and the cattle darting in front of him.

Despite the stampede, Diane fired again, the shot taking off a chunk of the steering wheel, but like her comrades, she wasn't aiming to kill, either. She wanted to take them alive. Or at least take Cassidy alive. And Sawyer had to figure out how to use that to his advantage.

"You're looking pretty fit for a woman who left her blood on that warehouse floor," Sawyer shouted.

"I am fit. Drew the blood myself and planted it there. I thought it would take me off your suspect list. No such luck. I also thought the fake robbery at the lab would get me off it. No such luck with that, either. You just don't give up, do you?"

"Never," he grumbled.

"You broke into the lab?" Bennie howled, still struggling. "You tried to set me up, tried to make me look guilty."

"You are guilty," Diane concluded. "Just not of that particular fake robbery." She turned her attention back to Sawyer. "I heard the conversations you and your cousins had at the sheriff's office because I planted a listening device on the front desk the day I visited."

A bug.

Oh, mercy.

They hadn't even thought to check for that. And it had allowed Diane to follow their every move. Sawyer quickly tried to go back through everything that had been said over the past two days. There'd been a lot of talk not just between Cassidy and him, but his cousins had also spent a lot of time on this investigation.

"You also put tracking devices on all the vehicles," Sawyer said.

"I did that as a precaution. And then I had one of my hired men go out to the Ryland ranch. He pretended to work for the electric company, and he tagged all the vehicles there. Just in case."

"You went to a lot of trouble for someone on the bottom of my suspect list," Sawyer pointed out.

"I might have been at the bottom, but I was still on the list. After I heard all the calls and speculation, I knew they or you wouldn't quit until one of you managed to piece everything together," she continued. "But here's your chance. Let's end this before anyone gets hurt."

"Too late," Sawyer shouted back. "Someone's dead." And he hoped that only applied to April. It was making him antsy that he hadn't seen hide nor hair of Grayson since he'd gotten out of the truck.

"April was a casualty of her own stupidity," Diane declared. She definitely didn't sound like the shrink who'd been in the sheriff's office. She sounded more like a cold-blooded killer. And probably was.

"You're blaming the victim," Sawyer snapped. Yeah, it was probably dumb to egg her on, but he hated this cold witch who had placed Emma and Cassidy in so much danger.

"April wasn't a victim," Diane argued in that ice-queen tone that set his teeth on edge. "She agreed to help set up Bennie's kidnapping."

All right. He hadn't exactly seen that coming, but with April's track record, it shouldn't have been much of a surprise. Bennie and April were criminals at the core.

And if he was to believe Bennie—and he did about this—they'd made Emma.

Inside, Sawyer cursed that. Not because he thought they'd passed on those criminal genes to Emma. No, Bennie had good genes. Like Cassidy. He'd just made plenty of bad choices with the good things he'd been given in life. But what gnawed away at Sawyer was that Bennie now had a claim to the little girl who Sawyer loved like his own.

"If April was on your side," Sawyer said, "then why is she dead?"

Diane shrugged. "Because she got greedy. Wanted a bigger cut of the ransom, and I wasn't willing to give up a dollar more than I'd promised her."

"And that's when you had her killed," Bennie shouted.

Diane certainly didn't deny it, and she turned her stony gaze in the direction of Bennie and the gunman. They stepped out, the gunman dragging Bennie closer to the truck. The man had removed his mask, and Sawyer got a good look at him. He was a stranger. A hired gun.

But what exactly was this gun supposed to do?

And where was Chester Finley's brother, Joe? Chester had already indicated that Joe worked for the kidnapping boss, and that likely meant he was somewhere out there. Hopefully, not putting a bullet in Grayson.

"If you hurt Cassidy," Sawyer reminded Diane, "you won't get a penny."

"And that's the only reason she's still alive." It was as if she had ice water in her veins, and that sent Sawyer's blood boiling. How dare this witch risk Cassidy's and Emma's lives for money.

"Cassidy will come with me," Diane continued, "and when I have the cash, I'll let her go."

"No, you won't." Sawyer hated to lay it all out there like that, especially since the color had drained from Cassidy's face. But Cassidy no doubt already knew what Diane had in mind—she wanted to kill them all so there would be no witnesses to her crime.

The gunman and Bennie stopped just a few feet from the truck. "Your cousin, you and Bennie will stay here," Diane ordered, and she motioned for Cassidy to get out.

Sawyer caught on to Cassidy so she'd stay put. "How was the baby involved in this plan of yours?" It was something he could learn later, but he wanted to buy some time. Maybe for Grayson to get into place. Maybe for Diane and her hired goon to let down their guard.

All Sawyer needed was a split-second distraction.

"Talk time is over," Diane snapped.

Sawyer shook his head. "If you want Cassidy to get out, then tell me why you had her bring me the baby, why you let me believe it was mine."

Diane's glare got worse, and she didn't say anything for several heart-stopping moments. "I figured once you learned the baby was Bennie's, you'd blame him for all of this. He's a good scapegoat."

"I didn't know she was going to use the baby. Or kill April," Bennie blurted out. "If I had known, I would never have agreed to the fake kidnapping—"

"Shut him up," Diane said. And her henchman bashed his gun against the side of Bennie's head. He went down to the ground like a rock.

"Don't worry, he's not dead—yet," Diane added. "But if Cassidy doesn't step out now, then my next order is to put a bullet in Bennie's head."

"I have to go," Cassidy immediately said. "I can't let him die."

Sawyer got that. After all, he had a kid brother, too. But he couldn't let Cassidy do this.

"If you think your cousin can help you, you're wrong," Diane continued, her voice more than a little smug now. "One of my employees has him tied up."

Sawyer had no idea if that was true, but just in case, he knew he couldn't rely on Grayson for help. Or Bennie. And that meant he had to do something now.

But *now* came a little sooner than planned.

Yelling like a man on fire, Bennie got up and although his hands were tied in front of him, he swung his elbow back and connected with the gunman's gut. The guy yelped in pain.

It was just the distraction Sawyer needed.

He leaned forward, putting the weight of his chest onto the horn. The blare got the cows moving again. And in the same motion, he took aim at Diane.

However, she fired first.

Not at Sawyer.

But at Bennie.

Diane's shot slammed into Bennie's chest.

CASSIDY HEARD HERSELF SCREAM, and she tried to get to her brother before he hit the ground. But Sawyer stopped her from doing that.

He pushed her aside, took aim at Diane and fired.

However, Diane had already moved out of the way by the time Sawyer's bullet made it to her. She dived to the side of some cows, out of the line of fire. But Sawyer and she weren't out of danger. Neither was Bennie. Because the gunman who'd been holding Bennie suddenly had his hands free when Bennie dropped, and the guy fired at Sawyer and her.

Sawyer pulled her down onto the seat with him but kept the horn blaring. It was hard to think with the noise, and it took her a moment to realize why he was doing that.

It got the cows moving.

Away from Diane.

And that made her an easier target. She must have realized it, too, because she fired a shot at Sawyer and bolted behind a tree.

There were so many sounds. The shots. The horn blaring in spurts. But Cassidy was able to pick through all of it and hear her brother. Bennie was moaning in pain. That meant he was alive, thank God, but he wouldn't be for long with Diane's bullet in him.

"Stay down," Sawyer told her. He threw open the glove compartment and took out a gun. He put it in her right hand and put her left on the horn. "Keep up the sound so Diane can't hear me when I open the truck door."

"No." Cassidy tried to make him stay put.

"Bennie needs an ambulance. I have to stop her." And he pressed a quick kiss on her mouth and scrambled out the passenger's side.

The movement got Diane's attention. She leaned out, ready to fire at Sawyer, but Cassidy took aim. Pulled the trigger. She'd never fired before, and she missed. But it forced Diane to dart back behind the tree.

Sawyer threaded himself between the cows, using them for cover, and made his way closer to Diane. Cassidy was so focused on him that the shot startled her.

The shot hadn't come from Diane or her henchmen.

But rather from behind.

The gunman fell clutching his chest, and that's when Cassidy spotted Grayson in the side mirror. He wasn't tied up, after all. He'd taken out the gunman, but Diane was still armed and just as dangerous.

She held her breath, waited and watched. Each time Diane looked out, Cassidy fired a shot at her. Her aim was still awful, but it got the job done. Diane was forced to stay put while Sawyer inched his way to her. But Cassidy was forced to stay put, too, and each step Sawyer took seemed to take an eternity.

Sawyer made it within just a few yards of the woman, when the cows bolted to the side, leaving him without any cover. Diane instantly spotted him and fired.

She missed. Barely. Cassidy thought the bullet came so close to Sawyer that he could probably feel the heat from it.

Sawyer spun away from her, and both Sawyer and Cassidy pulled their triggers.

The combined blasts were deafening, but as before, Diane had already moved before the shots could get to her. Diane pulled the trigger.

And her gun jammed.

Cassidy thought maybe her heart had stopped, and she froze. But Sawyer didn't. He lunged at Diane, and they crashed to the ground.

Cassidy hurried out of the truck, and she glanced at Bennie first. There was blood covering the front of his shirt, but he was alive. He motioned toward her, and it took her a moment to realize he was telling her to go to Sawyer.

"Help him," Bennie said, his voice weak. "Diane's a dangerous woman."

Cassidy was well aware of that. Diane was a killer and would no doubt do the same to Sawyer if given the chance. She hurried toward them and glanced behind her when she heard footsteps. It was Grayson, and he stopped to help her brother. Cassidy hurried on, and when she got to Sawyer, she saw him in a tangle with Diane.

The woman still had her gun.

And her finger was on the trigger.

She fired, and Cassidy could only pray that the bullet hadn't hit Sawyer. He caught on to Diane's wrist, bashed her hand against the tree until her gun went flying. Diane screamed and scrambled for it.

But it was too late.

Sawyer caught on to her and pushed her hard against the tree. In the same motion, he put his gun to her. "Give me a reason to fire."

Cassidy didn't think that was a bluff. Sawyer was more than ready to shoot, and she totally understood why. The greedy witch had nearly gotten them all killed.

"We need an ambulance fast," Grayson shouted, his voice tearing through the silence. "Bennie's bleeding out."

Chapter Twenty

Sawyer wondered if Cassidy would ever stop trembling. Nothing seemed to help. Not his arm around her. Not his assurances that the danger was finally over.

Assurances wouldn't stop nightmares though.

And Cassidy would no doubt have enough of those for a lifetime.

She lifted her head from his shoulder when they heard footsteps coming toward the waiting room at the Silver Creek hospital. But it wasn't the doctor. It was Sawyer's cousin Gage, who'd no doubt arrived for the birth of Mason's baby. It was the reason nearly all of his cousins were there. That, and to give Sawyer a little moral support for everything they'd been through.

"Bennie should have been out of surgery by now," Cassidy mumbled.

Yeah, he should have. It had been two hours, and while Sawyer didn't have a lick of medical training, that seemed way too long. Bennie could be dying.

Or already dead.

It wouldn't matter to Cassidy that her brother had helped set up the kidnapping. It would only matter that she was losing him. Even with all the wrongs Bennie had done, that would always tear away at her heart, and there was nothing Sawyer could do to change it.

Grayson finished the phone call he'd been making and turned in his seat to snag Sawyer's attention. "Diane's talking, trying to work out a plea deal before her hired guns do."

"Is she implicating Bennie?" Cassidy asked.

"Yeah," he hesitantly answered. "She says it was Bennie's idea to get the photo of the baby with Sawyer. They were going to use it to set up Sawyer for April's murder."

Hell, that wasn't easy to hear. "Diane could be lying," Sawyer reminded Cassidy.

But if she wasn't, it was a smart move.

April had been demanding a bigger cut of the ransom money, and in Diane's mind, she needed to be eliminated. Best to set up either Bennie or himself to take the fall for it. It wouldn't have mattered when later they'd learned that Sawyer wasn't the baby's father. This was all about casting suspicion, and the photo of Sawyer holding the baby could have set the stage for him to go after the woman who'd wrongfully accused him of getting her pregnant.

"Please tell me Diane won't be getting out of jail," Cassidy said to Grayson.

"She won't be. There's all sorts of evidence coming in on her drug use and extortion of some of her patients. Coupled with April's murder and the kidnapping attempts, it's enough to put her away for life."

Good. That was one less worry. Sawyer didn't want Diane anywhere near Cassidy again.

More footsteps, and they got everyone's attention. Sawyer expected to see Mason come through the door to tell them about his newborn, but it was Bree, Gage's wife, and she wasn't empty handed. She was carrying a bundled-up Emma in her arms.

That got Cassidy and him to their feet.

"I thought this little one might cheer you up," Bree said. Her slight smile made Sawyer believe his cousin knew exactly how much this baby meant to him.

Bennie's baby.

That reminder hit him like a fist. Sawyer didn't care what Emma's DNA proved, he wanted her to be *his*. He just hadn't realized how much he'd wanted that until now—when Bree slipped Emma into his arms. How the heck could Emma feel like his baby when she wasn't?

"Hi, sweetheart," Cassidy said softly. She leaned in and kissed the baby's cheek. Even though Emma was asleep, she lifted one lid as if peeking out at them, made a soft kittenlike sound and then went straight back to sleep.

Since Cassidy was still trembling, Sawyer eased Emma toward her. That got him a smile, and some of the trembling stopped when she snuggled Emma against her.

"What'll happen to her?" Cassidy whispered. The tremble was in her voice now. And the worry. It was the same worry that Sawyer was feeling.

"Her mother's dead, so that leaves Bennie to decide." Except he might have the decision made for him.

"He's facing jail time," Cassidy added.

Yeah, he was. Maybe he'd get a lesser sentence if he agreed to testify against Diane, but kidnapping was still a felony. And if April's murder got tacked onto it, Bennie might spend the rest of his life behind bars.

"Thank you," Cassidy said, getting his attention. "You saved her life and mine."

He didn't want her thanks. It only made him feel worse for not having protected them in the first place. Yes, they were both safe now, and thankfully, Emma had no idea what was going on. But Cassidy would remember.

The bullets. The blood.

The fear that no doubt had her by the throat.

"If I'd realized sooner that the culprit was Diane," he said, "I could have put an end to her dangerous plan."

Cassidy stared at him. And stared. "I didn't realize the FBI had issued ESP with your badge."

He frowned, shook his head.

"There's no way you could have known any sooner," Cassidy continued before he could say anything. "No way you could have stopped her before tonight. She was manipulative and greedy, and she fooled a lot of people."

Including him. "If she'd just stopped fooling me a little sooner, you wouldn't have had to go through tonight. Bennie might not have been shot."

She huffed. She didn't roll her eyes, but she came close. "Now you're taking the blame for Bennie? He broke the law, Sawyer. I hate that he was hurt, but we were partly in that position because of him. I'll forgive him for it because he's my brother, but I'll never forgive him for nearly getting you killed."

It was a concession that he didn't deserve. But he'd take it.

Sawyer leaned in and brushed his mouth over hers. She trembled again. Just a little. But he thought it was a good trembling this time. So Sawyer kissed her again, and this time he lingered long enough that Gage cleared his throat.

"Need a sitter?" Gage asked. It was an innocent enough question, but since he hadn't missed the kiss, it was really an offer for Cassidy and him to head off to bed.

Something that suddenly held great appeal for Sawyer.

Sure, they were at the hospital, waiting for Bennie to get out of surgery, but he wished he could magically transport Cassidy to another place.

Okay, to bed.

While Gage babysat Emma for an hour or so.

"You're smiling," Cassidy said.

Sawyer automatically fixed that. "Sorry."

It wasn't a smiling kind of situation, but it became one when Cassidy smiled, too. She opened her mouth to say something but didn't get the chance because they heard the sound of more footsteps.

This time, however, it was the surgeon.

Cassidy and he both got to their feet and went to the doorway. Sawyer didn't know the doc, and his poker face gave away nothing.

"Your brother made it through surgery," he finally said. "He'll recover, but he'll be in the hospital for a week or more."

Cassidy's breath rushed out. Obviously relieved. So was Sawyer. Cassidy loved Bennie, and he didn't want her to go through the pain of losing him.

"Can we see him?" Cassidy asked.

"Not for a while, but before he was sedated, he gave me a message to give to you." The doctor looked down at the baby. "Your brother said he wants you to have custody of her, that he'll do the paperwork as soon as he's able."

Sawyer's lungs started to burn like crazy, and that's when he realized he'd been holding his breath. Good. Bennie had wised up and done the right thing by handing over his baby girl to Cassidy. It was the best thing for all of them.

Well, except for him.

Where the heck did that leave him? Cassidy had the money and resources to raise a baby. The desire was there, too. He could see the love for Emma all over her face. So, why the heck didn't that make him feel like jumping for joy?

Because he loved Emma, too.

Ah, heck. When had his life gotten so complicated?

He was the Ryland who was immune to babies and fatherhood. His own miserable childhood had prepared him for that. But then Sawyer glanced around the room. Nearly everyone there had had a lousy childhood, and they'd all gotten past it and had become parents.

The surgeon stepped away, and Sawyer saw the newest father walking straight toward them. Not alone, either. He was pushing a clear hospital bassinette with the baby inside. Mason wasn't much for smiling, but Sawyer definitely detected a smile as Mason pulled back the blanket and showed them the latest Ryland.

The baby looked like a little boxer with his hands balled into fists, and he was flailing them around and making choppy crying sounds as if testing his voice.

"Are you supposed to be out here with the baby?" Sawyer asked Mason.

"The doc said I could for just a second and if nobody touches him. Or breathes on him. There're too many of you to cram into the nursery to see him."

That was the advantage of a small-town hospital where everyone knew the Rylands. Besides, there really were too many of them for that small nursery.

"His name is Max Quinn Ryland," Mason said. Not just a smile. The man was beaming now.

"He's beautiful," Cassidy declared, but Sawyer couldn't quite see it. Well, mostly he couldn't. The kid had a mop of the dark Ryland hair, but he could also pick out some of Abbie's features there, too.

"Max is here!" Nate's daughter, Kimmie, squealed. Despite the fact she'd been sound asleep just moments earlier, she bolted from her mother's lap and hurried to Mason so he could scoop her up for a better look.

Soon, Max was surrounded by oohing and aahing aunts, uncles and cousins, and it must have been his night for revelations because Sawyer thought of something else. That little baby with the squished red face and swinging fists would always be loved. Always have family. Would always have a home.

"Cassidy, I don't want you to raise Emma alone," Sawyer heard himself say.

Good grief. He hadn't intended to blurt it out like that, and he sure hadn't meant for it to be so loud. Loud enough for everyone to stop, look and listen as if waiting to see which foot he'd put in his mouth next. Rather than let them in on that, Sawyer led Cassidy to the other side of the room while the oohing and aahing continued.

She shook her head, probably because she hadn't understood what the heck he meant. "Are you saying you'll help?"

"I don't want to help, either." Heck, he was making a mess of this. "What I mean is, I want to do more than help. I want to make sure Emma has a home."

She nodded, but he could tell she still didn't have any idea what he meant.

"I'm in love with you," she said out of the blue.

Okay, so maybe she did have an idea where he was going with this. *I'm in love with you* was a good start.

Very good.

Sawyer pulled her to him, and despite Emma's being between them, he kissed Cassidy. A little longer than he'd planned. When he finally pulled back, they were both smiling.

Except Cassidy's smile quickly faded. "If you don't love me, then I'll feel like an idiot for saying it."

"Don't feel like an idiot." And he couldn't say it fast enough. "Because I do love you. It makes me crazy. Makes me burn. But I love you."

Now the smile returned. The kiss, too. Cassidy initiated that one and slipped her free hand around the back of his neck. Emma decided it was a good time to get their attention by cooing.

Which made the moment perfect.

"I think she approves," Sawyer said. And he brushed a kiss on the baby's cheek. "Will you approve if I ask your new mom to marry me?"

There was no way Emma could have understood that, but it sure seemed as if she did because she cooed again. It was so loud that it startled her and she jumped a little. Sawyer laughed, waited, but what he didn't hear was a yes coming from Cassidy's mouth.

He lifted his gaze, slowly, and met hers. "I just asked you to marry me." And his stomach knotted. His breath thinned. He even felt a little queasy at the thought of her saying anything but yes.

"I heard you," Cassidy said on a rise of breath. "I just didn't think you would ask."

Oh. All right. Plan B, though it wasn't the plan he wanted. "Then, we'll wait a month or two, we can spend more time together, and I'll repeat the proposal." Though he couldn't imagine having to go that long without an answer.

"No need to wait." Cassidy caught on to the front of his shirt and hauled him back for another mind-blowing kiss. "Yes. Yes. Yes."

By the time she made it to the third yes, she was practically shouting. Emma didn't cry, but she did look up at them as if they'd lost their minds. They hadn't. They'd finally found them.

"I'll take that as a yes," Sawyer joked.

Obviously, going to the corner for this conversation didn't mean it was private. His cousins broke into applause when he pulled Cassidy back to him for a kiss that would seal the deal.

Forever.

His wife. His daughter. His family.

* * * * *

Look for a brand-new miniseries from USA TODAY *bestselling author Delores Fossen later in 2014. You'll find it wherever Harlequin Books are sold!*